Typewriter Pub, an imprint of Blvnp Incorporated
A Nevada Corporation
1887 Whitney Mesa DR #2002
Henderson, NV 89014
www.typewriterpub.com/info@typewriterpub.com

ISBN: 978-1-64434-193-3

DISCLAIMER
This book is a work of fiction. The characters, incidents, and dialogue are drawn from the author's imagination and are not to be construed as real. While references might be made to actual historical events or existing locations, the names, characters, places, and incidents are either products of the author's imagination or are used fictitiously, and any resemblance to actual persons living or dead, business establishments, events or locales is entirely coincidental.

GW00640880

THE SUBWAY

JAE JAE

type
writer
pub

To my mother,
who taught me that giving up was never an option.

CHAPTER ONE

I hated riding the subway. Not just any subway either. The subways in New York City, to be exact. I hated those things with an unyielding passion. There were no ifs, ands, or buts about it.

Who wanted to ride in an underground train that smelled like stale play dough and old people? Maybe it was just me, maybe I was over exaggerating, or maybe I was losing my sense of smell, but that was definitely the smell that aggressively assaulted my nose whenever I stepped foot in a subway car.

I hated how crowded they were too. I would receive an elbow to the ribs or a hard shove from someone's shoulder almost every time I was forced to ride that thing. At the end of my ride, I always walked out looking like I just went ten rounds with a mildly ferocious ten-year-old.

There was never anywhere to sit. If all the seats were taken by the time I got on—and they usually were—then I would be forced to stand among the crowd of swaying bodies, where perverts would "accidentally" rub up against me. It was like a game of musical chairs where the loser would get felt up by a bunch of strange old men as a punishment.

As if all that wasn't bad enough, the ride itself took at least twenty minutes and I had to ride the damn thing twice.

Why did I have to ride it twice?

Well, that's because I lived right outside my school's district. So *technically,* the school bus couldn't pick me up from my house, but we lived close enough that I could walk to the subway station in the city and get a ride closer to school and walk the rest of the way every single day.

I was eighteen. I should have been riding back and forth in my own car but no. My parents, who were definitely using their parent logic on this, thought it would be better if I rode the subway every day, despite the fact that I kept reminding them that I was bound to be kidnapped, robbed, shot, or a mix of all three by doing so. I did live in New York after all. Worse things had happened.

I made it my job to constantly remind them that when they saw me on the news with the caption "Missing Girl" above my hideous high school ID picture, it was going to be all their fault. With all the money I spent riding the subway, I could have bought my own car by now, but did I? No. Apparently, I wasn't ready for that big of a responsibility yet.

This is where you insert the eye roll and dramatic sigh.

Basically, they trusted me to venture into a crowd of people that could easily be hiding serial killers and knife-wielding maniacs—I really needed to quit watching so much *Law and Order*—but they didn't trust me with my own car.

Parent logic.

However, what happened on that one day I rode the subway, that one day that was supposed to be just like any other, I don't think anyone saw it coming.

Not me, not my parents, not the unsuspecting passengers on the subway.

No one.

The day where I would really be in my very own episode of *Law and Order*, and unfortunately, I'd end up being the victim.

Lucky me.

*   *   *

Whoever decided to make an alarm clock sound like the siren for the end of the world was an idiot. If I didn't die from the small heart attack the stupid thing gave me, then I'd end up smashing Satan's creation against my nightstand.

I'm currently on alarm clock number three.

Lucky for my current alarm clock, I wasn't in a *complete* hostile mood when it abruptly woke me this time.

Groaning, I blindly slammed my hand down, knocking various items off my nightstand until I found the snooze button and rolled out of my warm bed, blankets and all.

I landed on the hardwood floor with a loud *thud*.

My mom's voice rang from downstairs not even two seconds after.

"Gemma, what was that?! You better not have broken anything!"

Yeah, Mom, don't ask if I was the *thing* that fell and possibly broke.

I didn't even bother getting up or untangling myself from my blanket to answer her. I just rolled over to the door like some sort of deformed giant baked potato and yelled, "It was just a shirt!"

"What kind of shirt makes that sound when it falls?!" she yelled back. I could almost picture the deadpan look on her face.

Did I leave out the part where I was *in* the shirt when it fell?

"Well, I'm fine anyway! Thanks for asking!" I yelled back down.

"Just hurry up! You're going to be late!"

There was a slight pause before she added, "Again!"

Groaning again, I sat up and threw off my blanket, making goose bumps instantly rise against my skin as I slowly made my way across the hall to the bathroom.

I even made an extra effort to drag my feet.

3

Who cared if I was late? Was I really missing out on something important?

Lord forbid I miss out on my science teacher teaching us that the nucleus was the powerhouse of the cell.

Or was it the mitochondria?

See? I couldn't even bother to remember.

And don't even get me started on the whole y=mx+b thing.

I'd *definitely* need that information later in life.

After showering and doing my basic morning routine, I brushed out my hair so it no longer looked like a bird had made a nest in it, and it fell in its usual lifeless sheet down to my shoulders.

I got dressed in a simple white long-sleeved shirt, black zip-up hoodie, and jeans that my mother had bought me for Christmas last year, claiming that they hugged the curves I had, but I was pretty sure they were nonexistent.

I'm sure she only said it to try and make me feel better.

She got an A for effort.

After slipping into a pair of Converse, I did a once-over in the mirror to make sure I passed the 'Acceptable to be seen by society today' test, which really just consisted of me making sure I didn't look like I had been living in a cave for the last three months before I went outside.

Satisfied with my look, I grabbed my backpack off the desk in the corner of my room and bounded down the stairs one at a time. I tried the whole taking two steps at a time thing once, and let's just say my face paid the price.

As soon as I reached the bottom step, the smell of bacon assaulted my nose, making my mouth water. Stepping into the kitchen, I saw my mom—her dark and slightly graying hair pulled into a messy bun—still in her pajamas, leaning over a frying pan full of bacon.

My dad, with his also graying black hair, was sitting in a chair at the kitchen table with a newspaper in one hand and a white

"World's #1 Dad" mug—one of the many I had gotten him for three Christmases in a row—filled with coffee in the other. He looked like a dad straight out of a TV series. Who even still reads newspapers these days?

He was dressed in a white button-up shirt and a black tie with purple polka dots—another Christmas gift from me—black slacks, and a pair of glasses was sitting on the bridge of his nose.

Walking over, I plucked two pieces of bacon off his plate and smiled sweetly at him as he looked up from his newspaper with his eyebrows raised.

"You weren't going to eat it anyway," I said in response to his look as I shoved a piece into my mouth.

I walked over to my baby brother, Aiden, who was sitting in his highchair with a bowl full of, for lack of a better word, slop. I hope he hadn't been eating that.

I ruffled his fluffy brown hair before I leaned down and whispered in his ear, making sure I was still loud enough so that my parents could hear me clearly. "If you want live to see three, I wouldn't eat that," I said, gesturing to the unidentifiable contents that I'm pretty sure had just moved in his bowl.

In response to my whispered warning, Aiden smiled up at me like he knew exactly what I was talking about. My dad chuckled and my mom turned around to glare at me.

I shrugged and kissed her on the cheek before heading towards the front door.

Before I opened the front door, I yelled over my shoulder, unable to stop myself, "Only eat the bacon, anything else and you have two options: hospital or the grave!"

I quickly ran out the door before my mom could throw the frying pan at me. I could hear my dad's laughter echoing outside before I shut the door.

My mom would swear up and down that she was a good cook, but after last Thanksgiving, I beg to differ. That year, we had pizza for Thanksgiving, so I think that pretty much explained itself.

I couldn't help but laugh, then instantly checked to make sure none of my neighbors were out and saw me laughing by myself. I continued munching on my last piece of bacon before I made my way down the sidewalk, the chilly air stinging my cheeks, and toward the subway, not knowing what exactly would be in store for me when I got there.

CHAPTER TWO

I was halfway through my walk to the subway station when my phone started vibrating in my pocket.

Pulling it out, I saw I had a text from my annoying but lovable best friend.

That was enough to have me frowning though. Not because she texted me, but because it was only 7:00 AM. She lived right next to the school so she *never*, and I mean never, woke up this early.

I expected the text to be a life-or-death emergency and read something like: *"Someone set my house on fire and now I'm homeless,"* or *"I took a ski trip and a freak avalanche paralyzed me from the waist down."*

But when I read it, it simply said:

Did you hear what happened at school yesterday?

I missed school yesterday because of a doctor's appointment, so of course, I had no idea what she was talking about.

Frowning, I texted back.

No . . . you know I didn't come to school yesterday. What happened?

Not even two seconds later, I received a reply.

Archer Daniels is SINGLE!!!

All caps, wow.

This was followed up by a gif of some random girl dancing on a table.

7

I couldn't help but roll my eyes. *That's* what she had to tell me?

If there was one thing Megan would wake up this early for, it would be Archer Daniels. Our high school's very own stereotypical badass, who just so happened to have every female in the school ready to collapse at his feet, and unfortunately, that included Megan. Poor thing.

Archer had been dating Avery Robinson, and what a perfect match they made. She was your basic popular girl with the personality—or lack thereof—to match.

Surprisingly enough though, they had been dating for almost a year now. So even though I couldn't care less about Archer's love life, my curiosity won and I texted back.

What happened with him and Avery? And why do you care? You have a BOYFRIEND, remember?

Megan replied almost instantly.

I'm just delivering the news. Anyway, Archer caught Avery in one of the old bathrooms with another boy and you won't believe who it was!!!

I *really* wished Megan was with me right now so I could slap her. She loved to let the suspense build up whenever she told a story. She was all for the dramatics. She could never just flat out tell you anything.

I tapped aggressively at my screen.

Who was it?

The instant reply read:

Cade!!!

I actually stopped walking, causing a lot of people to bump into me and shoot me dirty looks as I read the text over and over in the middle of the sidewalk to make sure I read it right.

Cade Phillips and Archer had been best friends for as long as I could remember. They went all the way back to preschool. As far as I knew, they had always been troublemakers together; they were like partners in crime. The milk to each other's cereal and all that.

They might as well have been married. To hear that *he* was the one that was caught in the bathroom with Avery was shocking to say the least. Unfortunately, I couldn't say the same thing about Avery. She *was* known for doing things like this, hence the name "24/7 Market" that I so graciously gave her because her legs were always open.

I mean, don't get me wrong, I had nothing against girls who liked a no-strings-attached kind of relationship, but when they start wrecking relationships by purposely hooking up with guys—who were just as guilty, might I add—that they *knew* were in relationships, well, that's where I made the distinction between harmless fun and homewrecker.

Was it mean to call her a 24/7 Market though? Probably, but it *was* true. I needed both my hands and feet and maybe even a few of Megan's to count how many *taken* guys that she had slept with, and those were just the ones I knew about. I'm not judging though.

Live your best life and all that.

I tapped rapidly at the buttons on my screen as I continued walking.

Are you serious?! What did Archer do when he caught them?

He literally exploded. There were lots of screaming and cursing, and he actually punched Cade in the nose. I'm pretty sure he broke it. There was blood everywhere. They had to pull him off.

Wow . . .

Yeah, it's like I always say, you can't turn a high school whore into a housewife.

I don't think that's how the saying goes.

I'm pretty sure it does. Anyway, I'll give you the good details when you get to school.

LOL K . . .

9

I slipped my phone back into my pocket, smiling at my idiotic excuse for a best friend and looked up to see that I had made it to the subway station.

It was crazy how a little bit of gossip could make time fly.

By the time I had paid and made my way into the subway car that would take me closer to school, it was 7:15 AM.

Sighing, I looked around and luckily found myself a seat toward the back and as far away from everyone else as possible.

I hated it when I went out in public and the public was actually there.

It was only after I had sat down and was about to pull out my pair of headphones, ready to expertly ignore everyone, that I realized who was sitting right across from me, looking like someone had peed in his Cheerios this morning.

Sitting there, arms crossed, and dressed in a black hoodie and jeans, was none other than Archer Daniels.

CHAPTER THREE

I didn't realize I was staring until a pair of green eyes met mine, followed by the harshest glare I think I've ever received.

Archer was looking at me with an eyebrow raised. It felt like he was asking, "What the hell are you looking at?" But of course, he didn't actually ask that. He just continued to stare at me with that irritated and confused look on his face. For a second, I wondered why he was still staring at me, but then I remembered that I was the weirdo who stared at him first.

Embarrassed, I quickly averted my eyes and turned my attention back to my phone and headphones. I could feel my cheeks burning. My embarrassment quickly turned into curiosity though.

Why was he riding the subway?

The last time I checked, I'm pretty sure Archer owned a car. A black Mustang to be exact. Unless he bought it himself, I didn't know what kind of parents bought their teenager that kind of car, but I wish I had them.

I put my headphones in and randomly selected a song to play, trying to still my wandering thoughts and preparing for the twenty-minute ride. There would be one more stop before the subway train reached its destination. I was hoping that I could keep my mouth shut and stop myself from asking Archer why he was here for the rest of the ride.

I closed my eyes as I tried to relax as best I could in the hard chair and leaned my head back with music blasting in my ears, fully intending to ignore him and everyone else on this train.

Unfortunately, my curiosity was still buzzing like a bunch of angry bees and my eyes seemed to move of their own accord. Opening one eye— like that would make it less noticeable—I glanced over at Archer once again and . . . he was *still* staring at me! Although this time, that confused expression was no longer on his face.

Instead, it was replaced by a *slightly* amused one.

He still looked like someone had peed on his Cheerios, but with the slightly amused look he was sporting, it made his expression seem like Cheerios weren't his favorite anyway. So even with his peed-on cereal, it didn't completely ruin his day.

I'm horrible at analogies, I know.

Focusing back to the task at hand, I frowned slightly as he continued to stare before I took one of my headphones from my ear. I couldn't keep my mouth shut any longer.

"What are you staring at?"

The words were out of my mouth before I could stop them. I couldn't exactly take them back, so instead, I left them out there and waited for his answer.

When Archer finally spoke, I'm not going to lie, it kind of caught me off guard and not for the reason you were thinking.

As strange as it sounded, I couldn't remember ever hearing him speak.

We've been going to the same high school for about four years, and in all that time, Archer and I had never crossed paths. He stayed with his group of friends while I stuck to hanging out with Megan, even if I did think that she secretly wanted to be a part of his friend group. I'm pretty sure she put in an actual application.

"Weren't *you* just staring at me?"

Was it wrong that I was secretly hoping that his voice would come out sounding like one of the chipmunks?

Ignoring my wandering thoughts yet again, I focused back on Archer.

"I wasn't staring," I protested, but it sounded like a lame excuse even to me. A blind man could tell that I had been staring at him, but I wasn't about to admit that to him now, was I? I had my pride, you know.

"What do you call it then?" he asked, raising his eyebrow again.

"Not blinking," I countered quickly.

Archer shook his head and fixed those green eyes on me again.

"Then why were you *not blinking* at me?"

I gave a frustrated sigh and suppressed rolling my eyes. "Why do you care? You should be used to girls stari—" I stopped myself short, realizing I had just almost admitted that I had been staring at him.

Hell would freeze over before I ever admitted to that.

"You should be used to girls 'not blinking' at you all the time," I quickly corrected myself.

There, that was better.

Archer was good-looking and he knew it. His hair that was the color of freaking exotic chocolate and evergreen-colored eyes were just part of the package. He had a strong jawline and a straight nose. His teeth were straight and pearly white, and his body, I'm not even going to talk about it . . .

I lied. Yes, I will.

One time in PE, the boys had to play football. Just like in the movies, one team was shirts and the other was skins. Guess which team Archer was on?

Megan and I had been running around the track with the rest of the girls when I heard her gasp like she had been deprived of air. She had latched on to my arm with strength I didn't even know she had and yanked me to a stop and pointed to the football field. I followed her gaze to see what she had been pointing at, and sure

13

enough, there was Archer in all his glory—in nothing but blue basketball shorts and white gym shoes. The rest of him was bare and, let me tell you, it *was* a sight to see.

While I prided myself in not drooling all over him, he *did* have a nice body. It was like the gods of Olympus had blessed him or something. His chest was tanned and sculpted with broad shoulders, toned arms, and abs. It was a crime for someone to look that good.

A mischievous grin played on his lips as he crossed his arms across his chest.

"Of course I'm used to girls staring at me. I'm asking why *you're* staring at me. You don't even throw me a glance at school."

That caught me off guard too.

He knew who I was then? I mean, I wasn't one of the ugly stepsisters from Cinderella or anything but I wasn't anything special that really caught boys's attention. People—both guys and girls—usually noticed Megan. With her long blonde curls and ocean blue eyes, she's exactly what you'd picture when you thought of a pretty girl, but me? I felt like I was just, you know . . . average.

I had to remind myself that I didn't care whether he noticed me or not.

"I was just curious," I said, breaking my own train of thought.

"About?" he prompted.

"Why you're here. Riding the subway, I mean. Don't you have a car?"

The mischievous grin left his face in an instant and was replaced with a taut look.

"That's none of your business," he snapped as he turned to look in the other direction.

Woah.

The switch was like something straight out of *Split*.

I could picture it now.

"That wasn't me, that was Patricia."

14

I was only asking why he was riding the subway. It's not like I had asked something personal like did he wear boxers or briefs, which I didn't care to know by the way.

Annoyance overtook my slightly shocked state. I curled my hands into fists.

"Who pissed in your Fruit Loops this morning?" I hoped those were his favorite if Cheerios weren't. "I was just asking a simple question." I folded my arms and looked down at my phone, pretending to be interested in it and not the glowering green-eyed nutcase with a personality disorder.

Out of the corner of my eye, I saw Archer turn his head to look at me again. He slowly unfolded his arms and sighed heavily.

He paused slightly. "Look . . . I'm sorry. I didn't mean to snap at you. I just haven't been in the best mood lately."

I wanted to slam my head into a metal pole.

Of course he wasn't in a good mood. He had caught his best friend with his girlfriend in the school bathroom. While that didn't answer my earlier question of why he was riding the subway or excuse him from being all pissy with me, I decided to take pity on him.

I turned my head back to face him.

"It's alright. I get why you're in a bad mood."

He frowned at me and gave me an expectant look like he expected me to explain how I knew about his situation.

"My friend told me about . . . what happened," I stated cautiously, not sure how he'd react.

I paused for a second—apologizing wasn't one of my strong areas—before I continued, "I'm sorry about what happened, by the way. I mean, if I'm being honest, you could have done a *whole* lot better than Avery anyway. You do know that she's a complete . . ." I paused again, thinking of the nicest way to tell him that his girlfriend liked to sleep around. "She's gotten around a lot," I finally continued. "And I mean *a lot*. She's been with more guys than I've flunked math tests, and let me tell you, I suck at math. I

15

still have to use a calculator multiplying anything higher than seven. I mean I'm not trying to judge her, but you'd think she'd get tired. You'd think that you'd need a break from all that fu—" I abruptly cut myself off, realizing what I was saying and who I was saying it to.

You see what I meant? Apologizing was just not something I was good at and, apparently, neither was making people feel better.

To my surprise though, Archer didn't seem to take it too badly. He actually laughed.

Well, it was more of a sharp exhale of breath through his nose but whatever.

I wasn't expecting him to find it amusing, but I found myself laughing along with him. A few people nearby gave us annoyed looks but we—and when I say we, I meant me—continued to laugh anyway. When my laughter died down and his small smile was gone, Archer rested back in his seat.

He gave a deep sigh before he spoke, "Yeah, I know how she is. She acted different with me though. She wasn't anything like how people made her out to be. At least not with me, but that obviously blew up in my fucking face. Of all the fucking people, the last person I expected to find her with was my best friend." His voice took on a dark and almost sad tone.

He really liked Avery and look at how she repaid him—by screwing around with his best friend.

Without really thinking about what I was doing or why, I stood up, setting my bag down on my seat and made my way over to the empty seat next to Archer. After sitting d\\own, I placed my hand on his shoulder.

He turned to me with a confused expression on his face.

"Look, I don't know a lot about relationships. I'm actually probably the worst person to ask about them, but I do know that if Avery cared about you as half as much as I think you cared about her, then she wouldn't have done what she did. Maybe it was a sign.

16

Maybe you weren't meant to be with her." I said the last part cautiously. I didn't want him snapping at me again. I really didn't have the patience for that.

Archer continued to stare at me with that same confused expression on his face.

I couldn't say I didn't feel the same way.

Never in my wildest dreams—or maybe it would've been my nightmares—would I have thought that I would be here on a subway train, having a heart-to-heart talk with Archer Daniels.

"What are you doing, Gemma? Why are you trying to be nice?"

Now that *really* shocked me.

The first reason was because of all the things I had just said. He went and asked me why I was trying to be nice. I wasn't pretending. It wasn't like I was a mean person. I was nice all the time.

Or at least, I thought I was.

The second reason was because I didn't think he knew my name. Like I said before, we went through high school without uttering a single word to each other. I knew his name because I couldn't go to one class without hearing it from one of the girls.

"What do you mean why I am trying to be so nice?" I asked, a little offended.

Archer turned so he was completely facing me.

"I mean, we haven't said so much as one word to each other throughout high school. Why are you talking to me now, let alone trying to be nice to me? You don't owe me anything, and if I'm not wrong, I was under the impression that you couldn't stand me. If you're doing this just because you feel sorry for me, then don't."

My mouth actually dropped open. What kind of reputation did I have? Did everyone think that I was some coldhearted she-devil?

"It's not that I can't stand you. It's just that I wasn't about to worship the ground you walked on just so I could get a chance to talk to you."

Archer was silent for a moment as he seemed to think this over, then he nodded.

When he spoke again, his voice was so low that I had to lean in to hear him.

"I don't know why I'm even telling you all of this, but as sappy as it sounds, Avery was the first girl I was really serious about. I mean, there was another girl before her but that had about the same probability of happening as a snowball's chance in hell."

A small smile played at my lips and I scoffed.

I made my eyes go wide as I put the hand that was on his shoulder to my chest and faked a gasp.

"What? There was a girl that *the* Archer Daniels didn't have a chance with? I need to meet her and shake her hand."

Archer glared at me but I could see he was biting back a smile.

"You're hilarious," he said sarcastically.

I smiled sweetly and nudged him with my elbow.

We fell into a comfortable silence, and I couldn't help but shake my head.

Archer noticed and turned his head.

"What?"

"Did you think that after all these years that we'd finally be talking? On a subway of all places?"

Archer gave another nose laugh thing or whatever it was he did that constituted a laugh and shook his head.

"No, but I can't really say that I'm disappointed."

He gave me a sideways look with those green eyes. I felt my stomach do a little unexpected flip and heat rush to my cheeks.

Oh, hell no. That wasn't good.

Maybe I had diarrhea.

I should go to the doctor's again.

18

Archer Daniels didn't just make me blush.

It was my life's mission to finish high school without falling under the spell that only Archer seemed capable of casting.

I was not about to fail now.

I quickly turned my head, shoving my hands into the pockets of my hoodie as I hoped that he hadn't noticed the reddening of my face, but I caught the small smirk on his lips before I completely turned away.

Dammit.

I was saved from this awkward moment when the subway train slowed and came to a stop.

Like this moment couldn't get any more embarrassing and awkward for me, the train suddenly stopping caused my body to sway to the left and my body bumped into Archer's. Since my hands were shoved into my pockets, I couldn't brace myself for it.

So instead, Archer ended up with his hands placed on my shoulders to keep me from toppling over face first into his lap.

Now, *that* really would've been embarrassing.

I felt my face heat up even more, and I knew it probably looked like a beet right now.

I would've said a tomato, but I hated tomatoes.

I quickly pulled my hands from my pockets and steadied myself.

I glanced at Archer from the corner of my eye. When I saw he was still smirking, I punched him in the chest.

I instantly regretted it. It felt like I had just punched a brick wall.

"What the hell? What do you eat for breakfast? Steel? That's not healthy, you know?" I asked, rubbing my hand.

Archer shrugged.

"That's all natural, baby," he said and then added an over-the-top wink.

I rolled my eyes and bit my tongue to keep from laughing.

Maybe, and this was a big maybe, Archer wasn't *all* that bad.

That didn't mean I was about to join his fan club though.

He could kick rocks and blow bubbles on that one.

However, our light mood came to an abrupt end when the subway doors suddenly slid open and, instead of passengers boarding the train, five masked and hooded figures made their way inside.

They were all wearing dark jeans and hoodies that concealed their faces. Each one carried a black duffle bag. Four out of the five figures silently made their way into the other cars, leaving just one behind. The lone figure stood in the middle of the subway car and dropped the duffle bag with a loud thud, gaining the attention of all the other passengers.

Silently, he reached into his pocket and pulled out a black handgun.

Screams erupted all around as everyone laid their eyes on the weapon.

You see?

This is why I hated riding the subway.

CHAPTER FOUR

"What the hell?" I heard Archer mutter next to me.

I barely paid him any attention though. I was focused on the psycho with the gun standing in front of me.

I felt the train begin to move again. I let my eyes wander to the left, trying to see through the window into the next car.

There was another one of the darkly dressed figures standing in the middle of the car, holding a wicked-looking knife in his hand instead of a gun. He appeared to be speaking to the group of people in that car, judging from their expressions. My eyes landed on an old man closest to the door that separated the cars.

As if sensing someone was looking at him, he looked to the side, and our eyes met. He had thinning gray hair and pale blue eyes. Wrinkles covered most of his face, and despite the reassuring smile he tried to give me, I could tell that he was terrified.

I couldn't blame him.

Screams were still ringing out around me, and I had to suppress the urge to cover my ears.

I couldn't think with everybody screaming in my ear.

A gunshot rang throughout the small space, causing me to almost jump out of my seat. My ears were ringing. When I looked up, I saw the darkly dressed figure holding the gun in the air with their index finger wrapped around the trigger.

Everyone was silent now.

"Now that I have your attention, I'd like to introduce myself." The figure pulled off the hood that had been covering their head and face, revealing a creepy flesh-colored mask with holes for the eyes and mouth and a shaggy mess of short and greasy black hair on top of his head. When he spoke, his voice was muffled by the mask, but nonetheless, I could still hear that it was deep and rough—like a smoker's voice.

"You can call me Dox," he continued.

I frowned at that.

What kind of criminal introduced themselves to their victims? I mean, I doubted that *if* I made it out of this alive and went to police that they'd have someone named *Dox* in the system, but still.

The fact that he had introduced himself probably meant that we were all going to die.

That didn't do anything for my crippling fear.

"Now, first things first, we need to get a few things straight. Any of you scream again, you die. Simple as that, understand?"

When no one answered, he shot the gun into the air again, causing everyone to jump but no one screamed.

"I guess you all understand then. This ride will go by a lot more smoothly if you all just cooperate."

"What do you want?"

My head whipped to the side to see which idiot just opened their mouth when Dox had clearly just told us all to shut the hell up or else we'd be getting a bullet to the head.

When I realized who it was, my heart thudded rapidly in fear.

Dox turned his fleshy, mask-clad face toward Archer and tilted his head to the side before he took a few steps forward until he was right in front of us.

He seemed to study Archer for a moment before he raised the gun and pressed it to Archer's forehead.

I couldn't stop the sharp gasp that escaped my lips. My eyes had widened to the point of pain, and my heart thudded harshly against my chest.

Archer, on the other hand, looked completely unfazed by it, like strange men held guns to his forehead all the time.

"How about you don't speak unless you're spoken to?" Dox said coldly.

He wasn't asking him. He was telling him.

Archer didn't bother answering. He just stared back into the dark eye holes of the mask with a cool expression.

I was just about ready to pee my damn pants.

"Have you lost your tongue now, boy? I'm talking to you. Now is the time when you speak," Dox said. His voice was starting to drip with anger.

Still, Archer didn't answer.

I saw Dox's finger begin to curl around the trigger. I turned to Archer, who looked at me out of the corner of his eye.

I shook my head, silently begging him to just answer the man before he got himself killed.

I had no intention of watching someone's brain being blown out right in front of me.

Archer focused back on Dox and sighed heavily.

"Well . . ." Dox prompted.

"Fine," Archer said through gritted teeth.

Dox lowered his gun and patted Archer on the head like he was a puppy who had just fetched the newspaper.

"Good boy," Dox said before he walked back to the center of the train car, and although I couldn't see his face, I knew he had to be smiling.

Archer clenched his fists until his knuckles turned white, and I quickly put my own hand over one of his. This time, Archer turned to look at me.

I shook my head again.

He really needed to calm down or he was going to end up getting us both killed, and dying was NOT on my agenda for today.

CHAPTER FIVE

Dox walked back and forth in the small, confined space of the train car, switching the gun from his right hand to his left, and then back again.

I wondered what he was planning. If he was here to blow people's heads off, then why hasn't he? I mean, I wasn't looking forward to it or asking him to, but I hated waiting like this, not knowing what he was thinking or what would happen next.

As if he could sense my impatience, Dox spun around and looked at me through his mask. It felt like he was glaring at me, but I couldn't really tell with the mask on.

"You," Dox said, pointing the gun at me.

I froze and clenched my hands into tight fists as I stared wide-eyed, not at Dox, but at the barrel of the gun.

"What's your name?" Dox asked.

I wasn't sure what telling him my name would do, but I wasn't about to question it when he had a gun pointed at my head.

"Gemma," I said quietly.

"Gemma . . ." Dox rolled my name off his tongue. I gave an involuntary shudder. I didn't like the way he said my name.

"Why don't you stand up, Gemma?" Dox asked kindly, but I knew just like with Archer, he wasn't really asking me. He was demanding me.

I was about to force myself to stand, even if it was against my better judgment, when I felt Archer grip my left hand, keeping me in my seat.

I glanced at Archer and gave him a questioning look.

When a maniac with a gun told you to stand up, guess what you should do?

You stand up!

Archer didn't bother looking at me. Instead, he had his eyes fixed on Dox.

"Why do you want her to stand?" Archer asked while narrowing his eyes.

I wanted to slap my hand over his big mouth. Was he trying to get us killed? Because that's the only thing he'd accomplish if he kept mouthing off to the man who was currently holding everybody at gunpoint!

Dox clicked his tongue before turning his head toward Archer.

"I thought we already went through this. You don't open your mouth unless I tell you to." Dox said the last words slowly, and I doubted he would remind Archer again.

"Archer, please . . ." I begged quietly. If all I had to do was stand up right now—even though I highly doubted it—then there was no reason to make things harder than they needed to be.

Archer glanced at me, then back at Dox. I could see his jaw clench before he slowly let go of my hand and I stood slowly.

"Obviously, your girlfriend has more sense than you," Dox said while tilting his head to the side.

I thought about telling him that Archer wasn't my boyfriend any more than I was his girlfriend, but I kept my mouth shut. Obviously, there were bigger things to worry about right now.

Now wasn't the time, and there was no need to entertain this sicko.

I slowly walked up to Dox and stood in front of him, waiting.

26

And then I waited, and waited, and then waited some more. It felt like I was in line at Disney.

He said nothing, just stood there staring at me.

Did he want me to stand up so we could have a freaking staring contest?

He was making me extremely anxious.

"Are we just going to stand here and stare at each other?"

As soon as the words left my mouth, I instantly wished I could take them back.

Me and my big mouth.

My eyes instantly darted to Dox's clenched fists. Before I could look back at his masked face, I felt his hand connect with my jaw, hard.

The force of his punch made me bite down on my tongue as I stumbled back from the impact, my hand covering my jaw.

The train car seemed like it was suddenly bathed in bright white lights, and I reached my free hand out to try and find something to steady myself. I could taste something metallic and salty, which I knew had to be my own blood.

"What the hell was that?!"

He almost punched my lights out that was what it was.

I turned my head slightly to the left and saw Archer standing by my side, fuming.

I didn't remember him moving.

"You need to do a better job of teaching her some respect," Dox stated before he took another step towards me. "Or I could do it for you."

Archer moved in front of me and put his arm out, keeping Dox from coming any closer.

Dox stopped a few inches from Archer and stared straight at him through the eye holes of his mask.

"Move out of the way, boy," Dox said, his voice deadly calm.

Archer seemed to straighten, and he squared his shoulders.

27

"No."

"I'm going to tell you one more time. If you don't move, I'll put a bullet through your head, then hers," Dox said, gesturing to me.

I heard Archer take in a deep breath before letting it out slowly and then, "No."

I saw Dox's fist fly forward and at first, I thought it was for me again, so I flinched as a reflex and took a few steps back. But then I saw Archer's head snap to the right and a bright red spot blossom on his left cheek.

I thought that was it. That he'd only punch him once, but when he began to bring his fist forward again and again and again, I knew he had a lot more in store. He wanted to beat him to a bloody pulp, and Archer just stood there and took the blows; blood started to slide down the corner of his mouth and a cut opened up on his now busted lip. He gave the occasional grunt as Dox's fist continued to make contact with his face but other than that, he kept quiet as he took the punches.

For me.

I could hear people gasp sharply or whimper, but no one screamed, afraid that they would be the next person to feel Dox's wrath.

I couldn't stand it anymore.

I did that stupid heroic thing they do in movies and flung myself forward and received the next blow intended for Archer. The impact knocked me backwards and into his hard chest. I had the same painful dizzying feeling as bright white and black dots flashed in my sight, only this time, it was ten times worse.

Archer had better keep his mouth shut from now on because two punches was all I could take today. More blood filled my mouth and I groaned in pain. I felt Archer put his hands on my arms to steady me.

"Don't," he said through gritted teeth.

28

I was about to protest. I wanted to tell him that I didn't want him getting hurt trying to protect me, but I didn't get the chance.

Dox lifted his gun and pointed it at me.

"Well, aren't you two sweet? Trying to protect each other huh?" Dox gave a dark chuckle before he jerked his head to the door leading into the next car.

"Move it, both of you. Now," he ordered.

Still clutching the left side of my face, I stumbled my way toward the door with Archer right behind me, one hand on my lower back and the other on my arm. Whether it was to keep me from falling flat on my face or just there to comfort me, I didn't know. All I was focused on was the pain, which seemed to be everywhere in my face.

As Dox pushed us forward, I wondered exactly what we'd just gotten ourselves into.

CHAPTER SIX

Dox pushed Archer and I through to the next car, where another one of his masked psycho companions was holding the blade of a knife to the throat of the old man I saw earlier.

I stopped abruptly, causing Archer to run into my back.

"Gemma . . ." he warned quietly, but I wasn't paying him any attention. It was one thing to hold *us* hostage, but the elderly? Who does that?

They were meant to go one mile per hour, riding their little motorized scooters around the grocery store, and somehow still manage to run into the shelves and knock all the food down. They were supposed to give you stale candy out of their pocket, and pinch your cheeks too hard, or even yell at kids to get off their lawn, but to have a knife pressed to their throat?

Words couldn't even begin to explain how wrong that was.

How wrong *all of this* was.

A small whimper caused me to glance to my left, where I saw a little girl who couldn't have been any older than eight with strawberry blonde hair pulled into two pigtails. She had two pink ribbons in her hair and she was wrapped in a pink fluffy coat. She was crying silently. Her eyes—which were red and puffy from all the crying—were wide with fear as she glanced at the old man before turning to the masked man with a pleading expression.

The old man was probably her granddad.

What kind of sick twisted person held a little girl's grandpa at knife point right in front of her?

I was about to take a step forward—which would have been pretty stupid on my part given that I could barely protect myself—before the guy holding the old man slid the knife across the old man's neck in one swift motion.

I watched in horror as a waterfall of blood rushed from his neck before he collapsed lifelessly to the ground.

"Grandpa!" the little girl wailed. A chorus of horrified screams followed her own. She hopped out of her seat and ran to her grandpa's lifeless body before she sank to her knees next to him, his blood slowly seeping into her white tights.

I stared, unable to move or breathe. I pressed the back of my hand to my mouth hard and bit down, trying to keep myself from throwing up.

I heard Dox chuckle darkly behind me before he began shoving at our backs again.

"Move," he growled.

Numbly, I put one foot in front of the other, forcing myself to move forward and tear my eyes away from the little girl and her grandpa. The image of the knife sliding across the old man's neck and the gushing blood was imprinted in my brain.

We made our way through four other cars before we reached the front of the train where it was being operated.

Dox opened the door, and I had to bite back a scream.

There, on the floor, was the conductor with a bullet hole in the center of his head.

Dox lifted the man up like he weighed nothing and threw him out of the compartment, where he landed with a loud thump, before pointing the gun back at me and Archer.

"Get in," he ordered.

I walked in slowly and my nose instantly wrinkled at the smell of blood. It was smeared all over the controls, like he had put up a fight before he died. There was also a weird-looking metal

31

device that had been jammed into the center of the controls; a spark of electricity would shoot out from its center every few seconds. I looked out the front window of the train as we sped past flickering light bulbs in the tunnel. I wondered where we were headed now.

Archer walked in behind me, and I saw his face scrunch up as the smell of blood invaded his nose too.

"I'll be back to deal with you two later."

That was all Dox said before he closed us in and made his way back towards the back of the train.

As soon as the door closed, I pressed my back against the wall before I slid to the ground and pulled my knees to my chest.

This couldn't be happening.

Archer knelt down in front me with his arms on his knees. He stared at me intently, probably trying to gauge if I was on the verge of a nervous breakdown.

I most definitely was.

"He just killed him," I whispered, shaking my head. "He didn't even flinch. He just slit his throat. Right in front of his granddaughter!" My voice rose and I think I was starting to hyperventilate. I took in quick shallow breaths and slowly started rocking back and forth.

This type of stuff only happened in movies.

It wasn't supposed to happen to me.

"We're going to die. Oh God . . . we're going to die." I was seriously starting to panic now. What would my parents do once they found out that I had been chopped up into a thousand little bite-sized Gemma pieces? Then, there was Megan. She would probably take it worse.

Archer snapped his fingers in front of my face and broke me from my horrid thoughts.

He placed both of his hands on my knees and spoke very slowly, "We're not going to die. Okay?"

32

My eyes started darting around as I continued to panic. "How can you say that? Did you not see what just happened back there? They killed—"

"Gemma, look at me." Archer's tone stopped me mid-rant. I focused my eyes back on him.

"We aren't going to die. Understand?"

I took a deep breath and closed my eyes, trying to calm myself.

I wanted to believe him.

More than anything else right now, I wanted to believe in those words.

I counted to ten in my head before I opened them again.

I looked back up at Archer and nodded slowly.

"Okay," I said quietly. "You promise me, then. Promise me that we won't die down here. Not like this," I said as I felt unexpected tears fill my eyes.

I didn't want to die. Not here. Not like this.

I watched him as he reached out and wiped a stray tear from my cheek before letting his warm hand rest there.

I didn't push his hand away like I would've a few moments ago before this nightmare began. Instead, I welcomed it, enjoying the brief comfort his touch brought me. I needed this right now.

"I promise," he said quietly.

I could only hope that he kept his promise.

CHAPTER SEVEN

I'm not sure how long I sat there in the small cramped space of the subway control car, rocking back and forth, trembling, and thinking about what Dox had in store for us, but my imagination was running wild the longer we sat there.

What if he decided to slit our throats like his sick friend had done to that poor old man? What if he decided to throw us off the train while it was still moving so that our bodies splattered against the tracks? What if he threw us in front of the train? Oh God . . . what if—

My horrible scattered thoughts were cut short when the subway lurched and rumbled against the tracks. I frowned and glanced over at Archer.

"We're slowing down," he said.

Archer and I stood up at the same time and peered out the front window to see that the train car was stopping in front of an old abandoned waiting platform.

A sinking feeling crept its way into my stomach as I watched us approach. Why were we stopping here?

The sound of the door sliding open made me tear my gaze from the window and on to Dox, who was standing in the doorway, his flesh-colored mask and gaping black eye holes staring at me.

A shiver ran down my spine.

He waved the gun in front of him.

"Let's go."

Archer took a step forward so that he was standing in front of me— which seemed to be his automatic position whenever Dox was around now— and stared evenly at Dox.

"Where are we going?" he asked.

I wasn't sure because of the mask, but I could practically hear the smile in Dox's voice.

"We're going on a little field trip. Now, let's go. I'm not asking again."

Slowly, Archer took a step forward and I followed close behind, not wanting to be left alone with this man. We passed through the doorway and Dox brought up the rear.

As we made our way through the subway cars, I noticed that they were all empty. I wanted to ask where everybody was but I was afraid of the answer I might get, so I kept my mouth shut this time and kept moving.

As we made our way through the cars, I ended up stepping on something wet and slipped, almost falling flat on my butt. I looked down to see what I had stepped in and saw that it was blood.

My stomach knotted up instantly.

It was in the same spot where the old man had his throat slit.

It was his blood.

There were smear marks that led in the other direction. Obviously, someone had dragged his body somewhere else. I vaguely wondered where, and I thought about his granddaughter and if she was okay.

When we came to the last train car, which was also empty, Dox pushed us toward the exit doors, which were already open.

We stepped out onto the old platform and my earlier question was instantly answered. All the people who had occupied the subway cars were now on the platform, all on their knees with their hands tied behind their backs with thick rope, set up in a line.

Dox's other companions walked back and forth in front of them, each one brandishing some type of weapon and each wearing a different mask. There was even someone donning a sheep mask. It would have been funny in any other circumstance, but right now, seeing some strange weapon-wielding psycho wearing a sheep mask just about scared me shitless.

Dox urged us on and nodded to one of his "friends." This one wore a Jason Vorhees hockey mask and was holding two pieces of rope in his hand.

Jason Mask stepped forward and grabbed my arm roughly and spun me around so my back was facing him before pulling my hands behind my back and tying them in a death knot that any boy scout would have been jealous of. The same was done to Archer, who gritted his teeth as the rope was pulled tightly against his skin.

Once Jason Mask was sure we weren't going anywhere, he pushed us forward at the end of the line of subway passengers, where we got down on our knees and joined them.

"Now that you're all here, the real fun can begin!" Dox began with a clap. "I'm sure you're all wondering why you're here, why this is happening to you, and all that other bullshit." He laughed to himself.

"The answer is simple really. You all have two choices. You can either live or you can die today. It's completely your choice. If you do what we say, you might live. If you don't . . . well, you'll find out soon enough because I'm sure some of you here are going to be stupid enough to try us." Dox's masked faced turned in Archer's direction as he said this.

A whimper and a sniffle came from my right. I glanced down the line of people and my eyes landed on the same little girl from before—the little girl whose grandpa had been murdered right in front of her.

She was crying and her small frame was shaking, whether it was from the sobbing or fear—maybe both—I didn't know. What I did know was that I couldn't let anything happen to her. She was so small. So innocent.

I made myself a silent promise right then and there. No matter what happened from here on out, I'd make sure that she got out of here alive, even if I didn't. Then, without warning, my eyes traveled to my left where Archer sat, glaring at Dox. He had promised me that we would both get out of this alive too, but that didn't look like it was going to happen. To be honest, I don't know why I even made him make that promise. Dealing with these people, I knew our chances of survival were slim.

So as I sat there listening to the little girl sniffle and watching Archer stare daggers at Dox, there were two promises of my own that I made myself: to make sure that little girl got out of here in one piece, and if I didn't make it, to make sure that I gave them one hell of a fight.

CHAPTER EIGHT

I watched in silence as Dox and his band of masked nutjobs began untying people and ushering them down onto the tracks of the subway.

"Now, this is how this is going to go," Dox began as he paced back and forth in front of the abandoned tracks. "The tracks from here on out are abandoned and farther down. They break off into a bunch of unused subway tunnels. That's where you all are headed."

You could practically hear the joy dripping from his voice.

My eyes widened at his words. Why were we headed there?

"We're going to be playing a little game of hide and seek if you'd like to think of it that way. There's only one exit in one of these tunnels that leads up and out of the subway station, but finding it will be like finding a needle in a haystack. If by some miracle that you do happen to find the exit, then you go free, but if you don't . . ." I could practically hear the smile in his voice. "And we get to you first . . . well, I wouldn't want to spoil the surprise now, would I?"

The man in the sheep mask stepped behind the little girl and untied her wrists before roughly yanking her up, causing a small whimper to escape her lips, then he pushed her toward the tracks where everybody else was nervously standing in a group.

I felt a pair of hands grab my wrists from behind; I turned my head and saw that the man in the Jason mask was untying my ropes. I quickly got to my feet, not wanting to be manhandled and headed towards the tracks. Before I reached them, I glanced over my shoulder at Archer, who was being untied by a man in a black ski mask.

Archer joined me right after I joined the group of passengers on the tracks.

Dox stepped forward so he was standing on the edge of the platform and looked down at us through his mask.

"You get two minutes. Two minutes and then the chase begins, and you better hope like hell that we don't catch you."

"Why are you doing this?" a male voice demanded.

I whipped my head towards Archer, thinking that he had opened his big mouth again but when I did, he shook his head and nodded toward my right. I followed his gaze and my eyes landed on a boy who was probably a few years older than me. He had shaggy shoulder-length blond hair, pale blue eyes, and a silver hoop pierced through his nose. He was lean and tall and had that whole skater look going for him.

Dox stared down at the boy, but it was impossible for me to tell what he was thinking since I couldn't see his face.

"I'm doing this to prove a point," Dox stated simply.

Like that explained everything.

"What point?" skater boy demanded.

"That I'm free to do whatever I please. You all live in this world thinking that you're safe—that you're protected. You think that the police, the firefighters, the army even, are all supposed to protect you and keep you safe, right? But where are they now? Hmm? Do you see anybody down here that'll give you a second glance if it means risking themselves?" Dox shook his head when skater boy didn't respond.

"I didn't think so. Today, all of you are expendable except for one, and that one person will be the one to make it out of here and deliver this message to your pathetic police. When they find all of your dead bodies down here, they'll see what a complete failure this entire system is."

Dox glanced down at a watch that sat perched on his wrist.

"You have one minute and fifty-nine seconds . . . fifty-eight, fifty-seven . . ."

In a panic, everyone took off down the train tracks. I glanced to my left, trying to make sure that Archer was still with me before I felt his hand on the small of my back, urging me forward. As we started to run, I tried to scan the crowd for the little girl, but I couldn't see her. People bumped into me and even elbowed their way past us, trying to sprint ahead.

A man, probably in his late thirties with dark hair, had a wild look in his eyes as he caught up with me and Archer. He was breathing hard, and before I knew what was happening, he rammed into my back trying to get past, sending me sprawling forward.

My knees smacked painfully against the train tracks. I felt the man's crushing weight on my back, pinning me to the ground. I gritted my teeth through the pain shooting through my knees and back as I waited for the man to get off me and continue running, but he didn't. Instead, he grabbed a fist full of my hoodie and yanked me up roughly, causing a shriek to leave my mouth.

"What the hell are you doing?!" I demanded as I tried to free myself from his grasp.

"Sorry, kid, but if those freaks get to you first, then that's more time for the rest of us." The man wheezed, trying to catch his breath. "I've got a family."

Like I didn't?

I literally lost all hope in humanity as the man spun me around and pulled his fist back, preparing to smash it into my face, but before he was able to, he was yanked backwards and fell hard on his butt.

I saw Archer standing over the man with his fists clenched, and as much as I would have liked to see him pummel the hell out of the douche bag for trying to use me as bait, I couldn't.

40

For one, the man was scared out of his mind and fear made you do crazy things, and two, we didn't have time for this. We only had two minutes, which were probably close to being up by now. Any second now, Dox and his friends would be making their way down the tracks, planning to pick off whoever crossed their path.

I reached forward and took hold of Archer's arm. "We have to go. We're almost out of time."

Archer glared at the man for a few more seconds before he backed away, and we took off down the empty tracks.

CHAPTER NINE

My legs were aching, my lungs were burning, and my head was spinning, all while I was running for my life.

It was like gym class all over again.

I glanced at Archer. There was a sheen of sweat covering his forehead, causing a few strands of his hair to darken and stick to his forehead. A hard look was plastered on his face, and if it wasn't for my obvious lack of stamina and lagging behind, I'm pretty sure he would've been moving a lot faster.

I really needed to start working out more.

If I lived that long, I definitely would.

As we continued running, my heart hammered furiously in my chest, and it felt like I was going to puke acid really soon. My hair was stuck to the back of my neck with sweat and I was extremely close to peeing my pants for like the third time today.

I started slowing down, and eventually, I just stopped. I couldn't keep going. I bent over with my hands on my knees, trying to catch my breath.

Yeah, this was definitely like gym class all over again.

"Gemma, we have to keep going." I glanced up at Archer and shook my head slightly.

"I . . . can't," I said through gasps for air.

"Yes, you can. Now, move your ass or I'll move it for you."

I would've scoffed if I wasn't dying from a lack of oxygen.

"Get . . . to . . . moving it then," I said as I swayed on my feet.

Damn, I was *really* out of shape.

Archer opened his mouth to say something else, but he was cut off as an ear-splitting scream echoed down the tunnel. I turned my head in the direction we had just come from.

The man we had left back there.

Another scream followed the first, cutting my thoughts short. This time though, the screaming didn't stop. It continued and grew louder. It was filled with pain and fear that sent cold shivers up and down my spine.

What were they doing to him?

Archer walked up in front of me and he gently pulled my hands away from my ears.

I hadn't even realized I had been covering them.

"Gemma, come on. We have to go. Now." I nodded, ignoring the pain I still felt in my chest and took off again with Archer by my side. The run was shorter this time. Suddenly, the tracks ended as we came to the tunnels Dox had mentioned earlier. I counted seven of them in all, all leading off into different directions.

"Which one do we pick?" I asked while glancing over my shoulder. I kept imagining Dox and his masked friends stalking down the dark train tracks and suddenly popping up behind me before dragging me down one of the tunnels.

"Pick a number, one through seven," Archer said quickly.

I frowned at him. "What?"

"Just pick a number," he demanded.

"Okay, okay. . ." I quickly glanced between all the tunnels. "Seven."

"Okay, so we'll take that one." Archer pointed to the last tunnel to my right and walked toward it with me right behind him.

Once inside, I had to start feeling my way around until my hands brushed against the cool stone wall of the tunnel. The light

43

outside the tunnels had faded and there were no lightbulbs—it was now pitch black.

I edged forward as fast as I could in the dark, trying to keep myself from tripping or falling on my face.

I guess I was moving a little faster than I thought when my face slammed into Archer's back.

Pain shot through my nose. I groaned, holding my nose while I took a few steps back.

"Could you warn me when you're going to stop all of a sudden or maybe move a little faster?" I whispered harshly. Totally hypocritical of me when he literally almost had to drag me to get me to move a few moments ago, I know.

"I don't know if you noticed, but we have a bunch of nutjobs that want to kill us who are right on our asses."

I heard Archer turn around, his shoes making a slight scraping noise on the ground before I shoved him in his chest.

I was only trying to get him to start moving again but I ended up pushing him harder than I intended, and I heard him stumble back a few steps.

"What the hell was that for?" he whisper-yelled at me.

Even though he probably couldn't see me, I crossed my arms over my chest and huffed in frustration.

"You're moving too slow. We need to keep going."

I heard Archer scoff before he spoke again, this time, raising his voice, mimicking me. "I don't know if *you* noticed, but it's pitch-fucking-black. I can barely see my hand in front of my face."

I stomped my foot in irritation. I did *not* sound like that.

"Whatever," I grumbled before blindly shoving my way past him and stomping ahead.

That was a mistake.

Almost as soon as I stormed past Archer, I tripped on something hard and went flying forward. I landed hard on my hands and knees in something wet.

Please let that be water.

Somewhere behind me, I heard Archer snicker.

"Shut up," I said through clenched teeth. I tried to stand up, but something was caught on the end of my jeans. I ended up falling right back down on my butt, splashing back in what I was just going to assume was water because I didn't want to think of the alternative.

"If you keep making all that noise, they're going to find us for sure," Archer said, trying to sound serious but I could practically hear the laughter in his voice.

There was nothing funny about our situation right now!

"I can't get up. I'm stuck." I felt around my ankle, trying to free my jeans from whatever they were caught in.

Archer sighed before I heard him shuffle around for a moment before there was a bright light shining in my face, causing my eyes to water from the sudden brightness. I shielded my eyes with my hand.

Archer lowered the light. I looked up to find that the light was coming from his cellphone.

My eyes widened. We could call the police! Why the hell didn't I think of using my cell phone earlier?

Archer glanced at me and like he could read my mind, he shook his head.

"No signal."

I frowned. "We should still be able to call the police though."

Even if we didn't have a signal, cell phones were still able to make emergency calls.

Archer pressed three buttons on his phone. Even from where I was sitting, I could hear that awkward tone that meant the call didn't go through.

I sighed heavily.

Great.

Archer knelt by my foot; I glanced back down at my leg and found that my jeans had gotten snagged on a sharp piece of metal jutting up from the tunnel floor.

Archer sat his phone down and freed my jeans from the metal. I would've thanked him if it hadn't been for that stupid smirk on his face.

Archer stood up and held his hand out for me. I swatted it away and stood on my own.

"Do you want to lead the way or should I?" Archer asked with that smirk still on his face.

"I'm glad you find this funny. When those psychos catch us and chop us up into little sushi bits, we'll see if you're laughing then." I folded my arms and stomped ahead again but, this time, a lot slower.

In a few long strides, Archer was back at my side. When I glanced at him, he was no longer smirking. He silently turned off his phone before shoving it back into his pocket, bathing us in darkness again.

"They might be able to see the light," Archer stated simply, answering my unasked question.

My only response was a small nod and then we continued in silence.

After a few moments of walking, the ground seemed to change. It felt like I was suddenly walking downhill. I broke the silence wanting to know if Archer felt it too.

"Hey, is the—" My question was cut short when the ground suddenly fell apart and was no longer under my feet; a shriek flew from my mouth as I started to fall into the darkness.

CHAPTER TEN

One minute, I could hear Archer yelling my name as I fell through the darkness, and the next thing I knew, my body was smacking against the cold hard ground.

I cried out as bolts of pain jolted through every inch of my body. Tears filled my eyes instantly and spilled over as the pain took over. I half-groaned half-screamed as I laid there in the darkness. There was a horrible throbbing pain in the back of my head and an awful burning and ripping sensation in my shoulder.

Why was everything happening to me?

"Gemma!" I heard Archer yell again but it sounded like he was really far away.

How far did I fall?

I felt a cough rising in my chest, but when I tried to release it, a painful wheeze came out instead. As I rolled over, I felt a warm metallic liquid fill my mouth.

Blood.

That couldn't be good.

I didn't want to choke on my own blood because that would be a really shitty headline for my death when they found my body.

Teen found dead. Choked to death on her own blood.

Trying to avoid that being my death headline, I tried to sit up.

That was a mistake that I instantly regretted.

As soon as I attempted to sit up, I felt an intense pain run across my chest and left shoulder, and new tears filled my eyes. I couldn't help but sob as I flopped back uselessly on the ground.

This was just great. I didn't have to worry about those nutjobs killing me because I was going to die from my own clumsiness.

I could hear the faint shuffling of footsteps. Suddenly, a bright light was shining in my eyes.

"Shit!" I heard Archer's horrified whisper.

"Everything hurts," I said through clenched teeth. It took an extreme amount of effort for me to even talk. Every time I blinked, it felt like someone was trying to rip my arm from its socket.

I watched through half-lidded eyes as he knelt next to me. He sat his phone next to him, letting the light create a small pool of illumination around us.

Another wave of pain rushed across my chest and shoulder, causing me to cry out again.

I felt Archer grip my hand and gently push a strand of my damp hair out of my eyes.

"I know it hurts like hell but I'm going to help you, okay? It's going to be fine," Archer said in a determined voice. I wasn't sure if he was trying to reassure me or himself, but either way, all I could do was groan in pain as a response.

Archer leaned forward. I felt him unzip my hoodie, and as gently as he could, he eased me out of it but even that small movement caused me unbearable amounts of pain and another sob escaped my lips.

"It's going to be okay," Archer said soothingly as he began to pull the collar of my shirt to the side.

If this had been any other situation, I would have been asking him what the heck he was doing, but all I wanted right now was for the pain to stop, so I let him do what he wanted.

48

Once the collar of my shirt was pulled far enough to the side so that my left shoulder was exposed, I heard him suck in a sharp breath.

I wanted to ask him what was wrong, but my throat had gone dry and I couldn't bring myself to speak.

"Gemma, look at me," Archer said softly but with a demanding tone to his voice.

I dragged my eyes to his face, which was mostly cast in shadows, but I was able to make out the bright green of his eyes.

"I want you to keep your eyes on me, okay?" he said.

I was about to ask him why but he cut me off.

"Gemma, I mean it. I need you to keep your eyes on me. Can you do that for me?" His voice held no room for argument, so I nodded slightly.

I kept my eyes fixed on his as I felt one of his warm hands on my shoulder while the other was placed right above my elbow.

"Just keep looking at me," Archer said softly. Before I could even try to respond, I felt an extreme amount of pressure on my shoulder from his hands.

There was an audible pop but I could barely hear it over the loud scream that left my mouth.

If Dox and his band of lunatics didn't know where we were before, they definitely knew now, but I couldn't think about that now.

I was practically wailing. I bunched my hand into Archer's shirt. I wasn't able to keep my eyes on him, and in a failed attempt to try and block out the pain, I shut my eyes tight. Then all at once, the pressure on my shoulder was gone, leaving behind a dull throbbing pain, but it had lessened considerably from what it had been before.

A sheen of sweat covered my forehead as I breathed in and out rapidly.

"Gemma."

I pried my eyes open slowly before looking up at Archer, who was looking back at me with concern etched clearly across his face.

"If . . . you do . . . something . . . like that again . . ." I said through my pants for breath. "I'll kill you in your sleep."

I saw a small relieved smile replace the worried look on his face before exhaustion took over and darkness overcame me.

CHAPTER ELEVEN

Have you ever woken up from a nightmare that seemed so real that when you woke up, you weren't sure if you were still dreaming or not?

Well, that's exactly how I felt when I came to.

My body was covered in a cold layer of sweat; I could feel myself shivering. I also felt a pair of strong arms wrapped around me, and that's when my eyes flew open, only to be greeted with more darkness. I started to panic and tried to sit up, but a dull pain in my chest and left shoulder caused me to cry out. I shut my eyes before flopping back against a hard wall.

No, not a wall, a chest. I was lying against a chest.

"Easy," a familiar voice soothed.

I groaned and opened my eyes slowly, this time, a small light illuminated the small space around me. Archer's worried face came into view, and I almost sighed in relief.

I thought I had been cuddled up with some psycho and then, just like that, I was panicking again, but for an entirely different reason.

While I wasn't cuddled up with some psycho with a knife, I *was* cuddled up with Archer Daniels—that was even more dangerous if you ask me. In fact, I had gone way past cuddling, I was basically sitting in his lap with his arms wrapped around me.

Nope, I was having none of that.

Trying to ignore the pain I was currently feeling, I tried to lift myself up and out of Archer's lap, slower this time, but he slid his hands to my hips and tightened his grip.

I turned and glared at him, mentally burning a pair of matching holes into his forehead.

"Archer . . ." I warned.

In the dim lighting, I saw him raise his eyebrows.

"Gemma . . ." he said, copying my tone.

"Let me up."

One corner of his mouth lifted in an amused smirk.

"Why? Does this bother you?"

I tried to keep my attention on his eyes as I answered.

I attempted to look down my nose at him although he was taller than me, even when sitting, so it didn't really work how I wanted it to.

"If you must know, then yes, this does bother me. Now, if you don't mind." I gestured to his hands, which were still firmly placed on my hips.

"If *you* must know, I actually *do* mind. You just fell down a manhole. The last thing you need to do right now is move. So you're staying put."

A manhole?

Forgetting my current position, I asked, "What happened?"

Archer stared at me with a blank expression. "You fell," he said simply. "I thought that was obvious."

I sighed in frustration. "I know that much, thanks. I'm talking about how long I was blacked out, how'd you get down here, and what's going on with my shoulder? It feels like it's on fire."

I reached up to pull the collar of my shirt to the side to try and get a look at my shoulder, but before I could, Archer caught my hand.

I looked back up at him with a frown on my face.

"What?" I demanded.

52

"Don't touch it," Archer snapped.

"Why not?"

"Because your arm popped out of its socket."

My eyes grew wide. "I . . . what?"

"You," Archer said while pointing at me. "Dislocated." He waved his hand in the air. "Your shoulder." He pointed at my aching shoulder.

I glanced down at my shoulder, then back up at him, then down again, before looking back up at him.

"Then why isn't it poking out or something? How come I'm not screaming bloody murder? How come . . ."

"Because," Archer said, quickly cutting off my questioning. "I pushed it back into place."

"You . . . what?" I couldn't string together a sentence to save my life right now, and I'm pretty sure I was making a complete fool of myself by acting like this, but I couldn't help it.

"Have you ever done that before? Did you even know what you were doing?" I demanded. "What if you put it back in wrong? What if you messed something up and I end up losing my arm or something?"

Archer shook his head and ran his hand over his face before sighing heavily.

"First off, if I had put it back it wrong"—he put his hands up and used air quotes for the last part, mimicking what I had just said to him—"trust me, you'd know, and second, do you see a fucking doctor down here or anybody else who would give a damn because I don't. So instead of just letting you sit there, I helped your ass, but if you want to worry about something like whether I knew what I was doing down here of all places, in the situation we're in . . ." Archer waved his hand around. "Then by all means, go right ahead." Archer turned his head away from me and stared into the darkness with an angry glint in his eyes.

For the first time in my eighteen years of life, I was speechless.

To say I was shocked by Archer's little rant would have been an understatement for a number of reasons. The first one was because—even though I hated to admit it—I knew he was right. If any of those people who had taken off earlier came across me, lying in a pool of my own blood, with my leg chopped off, and a horn growing out of my forehead, I doubt they'd give me a second glance if they thought it might cost them their chance of getting out of here. It wasn't like there was a doctor down here either. The second reason that left me in stunned silence, was the fact that out of all the people I'd expect to save my ass, Archer was the last person on the list.

Sure, he had stood up for me on the subway train, but down here, I secretly expected him to ditch me and make a run for it the first chance he got. So for him to actually stick around *and* help me after I fell . . . well, I didn't expect it at all, but he was still right.

I bit my bottom lip nervously. "I wasn't trying to make you mad. It's just that this obviously isn't the easiest situation to be in, and I'm really close to peeing my pants. I'm scared as hell, I'm hungry, and my whole body feels like it was run over by a steam roller. I didn't mean to snap at you. I know it's not your fault. I'm actually really grateful that you stuck around and helped me even though you didn't have to. It means a lot that you did that for me . . . and . . . and I'm sorry."

I jerked back a little when Archer whipped his head back so he could look at me, his green eyes shining in the dim light of his cell phone.

I swallowed nervously and stared back at him, waiting for some kind of response.

I froze when he reached up and pushed a damp piece of my hair behind my ear. My heart just about exploded and fell out of my ass when he let his hand linger on my face.

What was he doing? Didn't he know that there were people after us? Shouldn't we be running for our lives right about now?

I was even more aware of my position on his lap than I was before. This felt extremely dangerous. There was no way I should be sitting on his lap and letting him touch me. I needed to get up. We needed to keep moving

"Archer," I warned quietly, ready to tell him just that as he started to lean forward.

I know this boy was not about to do what I thought he was.

Our faces were a few inches apart, close enough so that I could feel his breath on my face, making my eyes flutter.

I was ready to raise my hand to slap his face.

His nose had just lightly brushed mine, and I had just raised my hand to make true on my promise to slap his face before an ear-splitting scream rang through the tunnel.

Something you should know about me if it wasn't already painfully clear: I'm a complete and total klutz.

The sudden scream scared me half to death. In a panic, I jumped and slammed my head against Archer's.

I groaned in pain while rubbing my forehead. "You have a hard head," I mumbled.

"Yours isn't exactly soft," Archer grumbled.

"Whatever. Help me up."

Archer furrowed his eyebrows. "Why? What are you about to do?"

"Didn't you just hear that scream? Somebody could be in trouble."

Archer coughed and he sounded like he was struggling to contain his laughter.

I turned to glare at him. "What's so funny?"

"You are. Have you lost your mind? For all we know, one of those masked freaks could have gotten to whoever that was, and they could be headed this way right now."

I shook my head and ignored him. I tried to get up again, but Archer placed his hands on my good shoulder and pushed me back down on his lap.

"Gemma, you can't do anything for whoever it is. Don't you watch the scary movies where the dumb girl goes into the old abandoned house because she thought she heard something? That's exactly how you're acting right now."

"Well, I don't *think* I heard something. I know I did and you heard it too. Now let me up."

"Why are you being so difficult? It's not like they'd help you if it was the other way around. How many times do I have to tell you that? Do you not remember what that man tried to do to you back on the tracks?"

"You can say it however many times you want. I have to go see who it was." I tried to get up again but Archer only tightened his grip on my shoulder.

"Why?" he insisted.

I sighed in frustration. Why did I have to get stuck with Mr. Stubborn?

"Because it could be that little girl. She can't make it down here by herself. Hell, we can barely make it, so just imagine how she's doing. I have to find her, Archer, so please *don't* try and stop me."

Archer stared at me for what felt like an eternity before he shook his head and suddenly shifted, then he stood up and gently helped me to my feet.

Archer silently grabbed my hand. I had to resist the urge to pull my hand from his grasp. Why was he being so touchy?

Archer shook his head and sighed. "Let's go then, Wonder Woman."

CHAPTER TWELVE

Another little fun fact about me: I might have a *tiny* problem with blaming people for stuff that may or may not be my fault.

"Ugh, this is all *your* fault!" I hissed at Archer as we trudged our way through what I could only describe as green sludge. My jeans were soaked from my calves down with the stuff, and I'm not even going to mention the smell.

Archer spun on his heels, sending a few droplets of the sludge flying. A look of disbelief and shock was plastered on his face as he stared at me with wide eyes.

"Are you serious right now?! How the hell is any of this my fault? You're the one who decided to go all Velma Dinkley and wanted to investigate. Remember?" Archer raised his voice a few octaves, trying to mimic my voice again. "I'm going, Archer, so *don't* try to stop me."

I folded my arms and glared at him in the dim light that was cast by the old flickering light bulbs on the tunnel walls.

"First of all, if I was anybody from *Scooby Doo*, it'd definitely be Shaggy, not Velma, and second, you should've tried harder to convince me to stay." I took a few steps forward until I was standing in front of him. I reached up and knocked on his forehead with my fist before he swatted my hand away.

"If there was a brain up there, you would've found a way to keep me from going. So yes, this is your fault," I stated simply.

Yes, I know my logic was horrible. I told you I had a problem.

Archer's jaw dropped for a few seconds before he simply shook his head. "You're impossible," he grumbled.

I tilted my head to the side all of sudden and stared at Archer with a frown on my face.

"What?" he asked, glancing over his shoulder like he expected someone to be standing behind him.

It was like a light bulb had just appeared over my head and I snapped my fingers. "I got it!"

Archer turned his head back to face me and it was his turn to frown. "Got what?"

"You're definitely Scrappy."

Archer stared at me with a blank expression for a few moments before he leaned down so that he was at the same eye level with me.

"There's no easy way to say this . . ." Archer's voice took on a serious tone. "But you're an idiot."

I narrowed my eyes at him before I slapped his hands. "Let's just keep moving."

Archer shook his head at me before we continued down the tunnel. When the tunnel finally ended, it opened out into a large cavernous room. It was made of the same gray stone as the rest of the tunnels down here; jagged pieces of rock and pipe jutted up from the floor and hung from the ceiling.

There were a few pale-yellow flickering lanterns that cast an eerie glow across the large room, which meant that someone had been down here recently.

I took a few steps into the room and spun in a circle, looking around.

It was empty.

There was no other way in or out of the room besides the way we had come.

"There's nobody here, Gemma. We should head back and try and find our way out of here while we still can." Archer's voice rang out in an echo around the vast room.

I wanted to argue that we should stay and keep looking but there was nowhere else to look in here.

I sighed heavily before turning back to face Archer. I was about to agree to leave when the same shrill scream from earlier rang out from behind me.

I let out a startled yelp and spun around, frantically searching the room. Archer was by my side in an instant.

"Who the hell—" Archer started before he was cut off by the sound of shoes hitting the stone.

I whipped my head to the right where I caught a glimpse of black boots in the shadows of the room where the dim lighting didn't quite reach.

The boots began to step forward, revealing black jeans and then a black hoodie before finally revealing a figure donning a sheep mask.

My heart practically jumped out of my chest as my eyes took in the figure standing before me.

I took a step back before my back bumped into Archer's chest. I instantly felt him wrap an arm around my waist protectively before he pulled me behind him.

"You two are just too easy," Sheep Mask drawled out, his deep voice slightly muffled by his mask.

I frowned, wondering what he was talking about before the same scream rang out yet again.

My eyes instantly scanned the room looking for the source of the scream before Sheep Mask lifted his right hand. My eyes landed on the small silver device in his hand.

Sheep Mask pressed a button on the device and the scream sounded off again.

It was . . .

"It's a recorder," Archer spoke up.

"Gold star for you," Sheep Mask said mockingly.

I shook my head, still unable—or maybe unwilling—to put the pieces together.

"Why would—"

"So I could lure you two here, that's why," Sheep Mask interrupted and answered my unasked question. "I knew somebody would be dumb enough to fall for it."

Sheep Mask took a slow step forward before slowly tilting his head to the side.

"The really important question now is, now that I have you two here, which one of you is going to die first?"

"*. . . Which one of you is going to die first?*"

Those words bounced around inside my head as I stood there frozen, waiting for Sheep Mask to make the first move that would probably mean my death.

Another horrible thought soon joined the first.

If I made a run for it now, I might be able to make it out of here.

I quickly dismissed the thought, feeling terrible for even thinking about it. There was no way I was going to leave Archer, especially not after what he'd done for me. I'd made myself a promise that I planned to see through.

Sheep Mask took a step forward instantly, snapping me out of my thoughts. He cocked his head to the side and spread his arms wide.

"Well? Who's it going to be?" Sheep Mask reached into the waistband of his dark jeans and pulled out a black handgun. Slowly, like he had all the time in the world—which I guess he did—he took the safety off and aimed it at my head, sending new waves of raw fear coursing through me.

Out of the corner of my eye, I saw Archer tense and clench his fists.

"You, pretty girl?" Sheep Mask asked, amusement clear in his voice.

"Or . . ." He swept his arm to the left, now aiming it at Archer. "The wannabe badass? I saw your little hero routine you tried to pull off earlier on the train. I wasn't impressed." The amusement was gone from his voice and was replaced with an almost animalistic growl.

To my surprise, Archer spoke up, his voice calm and cold.

"You and your batshit crazy friends are the ones calling all the shots, right? So why don't you tell me? It's not like you were going to give us a real choice anyway."

I momentarily forgot about Sheep Mask and whipped my head to look at Archer with wide eyes.

What was his problem?!

My small hope of making it out of here alive went straight down the drain.

Sheep Mask tightened his grip on the gun and took a step towards Archer.

"I guess it's decided then," He hissed through the mask.

Archer shrugged his shoulders. "I guess it is. Just try not to get blood on my hoodie, it's new."

Sheep Mask actually laughed, a loud dark rumbling sound that filled the cavernous room.

"Try not to get blood on your new hoodie?" Sheep Mask shook his head, amusement now back in his voice. "Sorry to break it to you, kid, but that can't be helped when there's a bullet in your chest."

Archer raised an eyebrow in challenge.

"I never said it was going to be *my* blood." And as soon as the words left his mouth, he lunged forward.

CHAPTER THIRTEEN

First, Sheep Mask was standing with the gun pointed at Archer, ready to blow his brains all over the place as Archer stupidly stood there and provoked him, and the next thing I knew, Archer was on top of him, both of them struggling to gain control of the gun.

I watched in horror as Sheep Mask began to gain the upper hand and started angling the gun toward Archer's chest as his finger slowly curled around the trigger.

I made a split-second decision. Instead of just standing there like the idiots in the movies who just screamed and pointed, I rushed forward and brought my foot down as hard as I could on Sheep Mask's face.

He grunted and the blow was enough to make him loosen his grip on the gun. Archer took this as an opportunity to snatch it out of his hand. He rammed his knee into Sheep Mask's face before pinning him to the ground with his left hand around his throat. Using his other hand, he pressed the gun to Sheep Mask's forehead.

Archer took a steadying breath as he glared down at Sheep Mask with a hard look on his face.

"So who's going to shoot who?" Archer taunted.

To my surprise, Sheep Mask actually started laughing.

Apparently, it surprised Archer too because he frowned and asked, "What the hell are you laughing at?"

Sheep Mask continued to laugh for a few more seconds before he got his laughter under control. "You two . . . you just don't get it, do you?"

When neither of us answered, he continued, "Even if you kill me, you won't make it out of here. You can't. They'll find you. You're lucky I'm the one who found you first. I like to make it quick, but the others, especially Dox . . ." Sheep Mask shook his head. "They like to savor their kills. They'll make it slow and painful." Sheep Mask turned his head so he was facing me.

"Dox would just love to get his hands on you. After that little episode on the train, I wouldn't be surprised if he ignored everyone else down here just so he could get to you." Sheep Mask cocked his head to one side and was silent for a moment before he continued, "I wonder how he'll do it. Even for me, Dox is a pretty twisted guy. Will he carve up that pretty face of yours? Will he put enough bullets in you until you just eventually choke on your own blood? Oh, I know. He's been doing a lot of research lately, so he's gotten really creative. He's got a lot of wicked ideas. He'll probably tie you up and leave you in one of these tunnels. He'll place small little cuts all over your body, deep enough that you bleed but not so deep that you'll bleed out. You'll sit there until the rats smell the blood and come and eat you alive. It'll start with just one or two of them, then before you know it, there'll be hundreds of them, all feasting on that pretty face of yours. Your eyes, your—"

"Shut the fuck up!" Archer yelled, pressing the barrel of the gun harder into Sheep Mask's forehead.

"If you say one more word, I swear I'll blow your fucking brains all over this floor," Archer warned. There was so much hard venom in his voice that Sheep Mask was actually quiet . . .

But only for about half a second.

"What? You don't like to hear about all the creative ways she could die? I bet Dox is gonna make you watch. How would you like to watch her get eaten alive by a bunch of rats while you sit there uselessly, unable to do a damn thing about it? Hmm?"

63

I couldn't take it anymore. I rushed to the other side of the room before falling on my hands and knees. There was barely anything in my stomach so all I could do was dry heave. My body was shaking with cold shivers, and a cold sweat had broken out across my forehead again. This was too much. There was no way I was going to make it out of here alive.

I faintly heard a loud crack. Out of the corner of my eye, I saw Archer ram the butt of the gun into the side of Sheep Mask's face, effectively knocking him out and shutting him up.

I heard Archer walk up beside me before he knelt down next to me and silently pulled me into his chest. He rubbed his hand in small soothing circles across my back, and I let him as I buried my head in his shoulder. Silent tears ran down my cheeks, which eventually turned into ugly sobs.

I don't think I had ever cried this much in my life.

At some point, I was gasping for breath; I was pretty sure I looked like an ugly fish but I couldn't help it or even bring myself to care.

Archer gently pushed me back and held me at arm's length so he could look at me.

"Gemma, do you remember what I promised you back in the subway?"

After a few more sobs and loud sniffles, I shook my head slowly.

"I promised you that we'd get out of here alive. You're not going to die down here. Do you understand?"

When I didn't answer, he tilted my chin up so I was forced to look at him.

"Gemma, do you understand? I'm not going to let you die down here. You're getting out of here."

At that moment, I wanted more than anything to believe him, but there was that little voice in the back of my head that was stating the obvious.

There were only two of us and five of them. We were outnumbered. If we ran into more than one of them, we were done for. No matter what Archer said or believed, he couldn't protect me against all of them, especially if Dox had his eyes set on me now.

CHAPTER FOURTEEN

"What do we do about him?" I asked quietly, gesturing towards Sheep Mask, who still laid unconscious on the ground a few feet away.

Archer glanced over his shoulder at him before turning back to face me with a look of disgust on his face.

"I should kill him."

My eyes widened. While I hated the guy like I hated Monday mornings, I didn't think I could live with something like that on my conscience.

I shook my head. "Let's just leave him."

Archer scoffed and rolled his eyes. "What? Are you feeling sorry for him now? If you don't remember, he just tried to kill us."

"And killing him would make us no better than him," I shot back.

"This isn't the time for morality. Right now, it's kill or be killed. I don't know about you but I don't plan on dying down here. So you need to suck it up and get over it if you want to live," Archer all but yelled in my face.

My eyes widened even farther at Archer's words before anger quickly took over, and I narrowed my eyes at him. I took a few bold steps forward until we were only a few inches apart. I jabbed my finger into his hard chest before saying, "I don't know what crawled up your ass but you need to pull it out and calm the fuck down. I haven't been in many life-threatening situations, especially ones where maniacs run around playing dress up and trying to kill people! So excuse me if I have a hard time getting used to the idea of killing somebody! It might come as a shocker, but I've never done it before! But by all means . . ." I swept my arm forward in a grand gesture. "If you want to go shooting people left and right like it's nothing, be my guest!"

I spun on my heel after catching a glimpse of Archer's stunned expression and marched straight for the tunnel.

A few seconds later, I heard Archer's hurried footsteps behind me before I felt his hand on my shoulder.

I shook his hand away and kept on stomping forward into the tunnel, sending the green sludge flying everywhere, but I didn't really care. I hoped some of it flew into his stupid mouth.

"Gemma, wait," Archer called after me but being the stubborn person that I was, I ignored him and kept on going.

I heard him sigh heavily behind me.

"Do you even know where you're going?"

I glanced over my shoulder, shooting him a glare before I faced forward again. "Yeah, wherever you're not."

"You can't seriously be mad at me." Archer scoffed, which only caused my temper to flare even more.

I spun around and shoved his chest hard.

The steroid-eating-goober didn't even budge. He did, however, look pretty surprised.

"I *am* mad at you. I mean, I'm all for knocking the shit out of people but *killing* somebody? I can't do that and you just threw it in my face like I'm supposed to be able to do something like that. I've never killed anybody, Archer! Maybe that type of stuff is easy for a *badass* like yourself, but not for me," I huffed and was fully prepared to turn back around and continue angrily making my way through the tunnels, but I felt Archer grab my wrist and pull me forward so I collided with his chest.

My breath hitched and my heart was suddenly hammering in my chest. With my previous anger momentarily forgotten, I looked up into those green eyes and swallowed hard as I saw his intense expression.

Hmm. So *that's* how he got all those girls to fall at his feet . . . or on his bed.

His eyes were dangerous.

Two green pools of *"I can get you in my bed with just this look."*

"W-what are you doing?" I cursed my voice for sounding so weak.

Be strong!

Archer stared at me for a few more seconds before he replied in a low voice, "I'd never ask you to do something you didn't want to."

I swallowed again. "Well, sorry to break it to you but you kind of just did back there."

A corner of Archer's mouth twitched like he was trying to suppress a smile.

I dared him to smile. I'd slap it off his face faster than I swipe my card at Starbucks.

"No, if I remember correctly, I told you to suck it up. I was going to be the one to do it."

Asshole.

I scoffed and pulled back, giving myself some much needed breathing room. "That's no better. That's like kicking a puppy and telling someone to be okay with it."

Archer just shook his head at me.

"No, it's more like seeing a lion running at you, ready to have your little ass for dinner, and even though you love animals, you need to choose between letting it live or killing it to save yourself."

I stared at him with a blank expression before shaking my head and turning around to continue down the tunnel.

"That's a stupid analogy."

"How?" Archer demanded as he fell into step beside me.

"Because everybody knows that all I'd have to do is break into a song and dance to befriend it. Haven't you watched *The Lion King*?"

Archer was silent for a moment before he burst into a fit of laughter. He even went as far as bending over and clutching his ribs like anything I had just said was even remotely funny.

I was being completely serious.

When his laughter finally died down, he looked back up at me with an amused expression on his face.

"That is not how *The Lion King* went. There weren't even any humans in the movie."

I scoffed, shaking my head. "I've watched it over a million times. I think I know how the movie went," I said in a serious tone.

I heard Archer chuckle behind me before he slung his arm around my shoulder, being careful not to touch my other injured one, like we were old pals or something, and even though I should have punched him in the stomach for it, I let it go.

Archer sighed before glancing down at me. "What am I going to do with you?"

"You could start by finding the exit and getting me the hell out of here, then you could do whatever you want with me," I teased.

I didn't realize just how dirty that sounded until I actually said it out loud. Archer seemed to take my teasing a little too seriously for my liking, as I saw him give me *that* look. He didn't even bother trying to hide it.

Boys.

Men.

Hell, the male species in general.

We were fighting for our lives down here and his mind was in the gutter.

"I'm holding you to that," he said as he turned and led the way down the tunnel.

CHAPTER FIFTEEN

All that Archer had managed to do after he led us out of the tunnel was get us completely lost. At least when we started out, I was sure what direction we were headed in. Now, I had no idea.

"Your navigating skills suck," I commented as we made yet another left turn down another tunnel that looked just like the last one we'd turned into.

"Well, Dora, how about you pull out your map and lead the way then?" Archer snapped.

"I would but I left my backpack with Boots. Sorry," I shot back.

Archer groaned in frustration before he stopped and turned to face me. "What is your problem?"

I stopped walking to look up at him. "I'll tell you mine when you tell me yours."

Archer threw his hands up in exasperation.

"What are you talking about? I don't have a problem. All you've done since we've been down here is blame me, complain, scream, cry, blame me some more, get mad, get hurt and then blame me again."

I narrowed my eyes as my temper started to flare.

Again.

It seemed to do that a lot when Archer was involved.

One minute, we were throwing jokes back and forth, and the next, I wanted to shove my fist down his throat.

"Oh, I'm sorry if me falling twenty feet and almost turning myself into a scrambled egg was an inconvenience to you. Maybe if I wasn't stuck down here with a stupid stuck-up prick, who only managed to get us lost, then I wouldn't have a reason to complain."

Archer stared at me with disbelief clear on his face.

"Oh, is that all I've done?" he asked in a mocking tone.

"So let's just ignore the part where I saved your ass. *Twice*," he said, holding up two fingers.

I rolled my eyes at that. "I never said you didn't. I told you I was grateful, but this new situation we've found ourselves in is definitely on you."

"Once again, how is it my fault?"

"If you hadn't ran your mouth off to Dox, maybe he wouldn't be set on trying to kill just us, or more specifically, me. Or better yet, if you would've just kept a tighter leash on that stupid thing that you called your girlfriend, then you wouldn't have been down here in—" I was cut off when Archer stormed forward and roughly grabbed my arm, slamming my back into the tunnel wall and pinning me there.

Too much?

I stared up at him with wide eyes as he stared down at me, fury swimming in his eyes.

"Don't," he warned. "You don't know what you're talking about," he ground out between clenched teeth.

My initial shock quickly wore off.

"I normally wouldn't say this but you're seriously whipped. She was out there screwing your best friend and you're *still* trying to defend her? Even when it's clear that she doesn't give a rat's ass about you? Archer, you need to open your eyes. What she did with Cade is what she does best. You really need to start picking your best friends and girlfriends better."

I watched as the muscles in his jaw clenched. I could actually feel his anger as his grip on my arm tightened to the point of pain, which caused me to wince.

I glanced down at his hands and then back up at him. "Archer, let go. You're hurting me."

He blinked twice before he glanced down at his hand that was still clamped down on my arm as if he just realized it was there.

He quickly pulled his hand back and shoved both of them into his pockets. He backed up a few steps and took a deep breath, keeping his eyes on the ground.

I stood there, watching him as I absentmindedly reached up to rub my arm. This caught his attention as his eyes snapped to the hand that was rubbing my arm. As soon as I noticed him staring, I dropped my hand.

Without uttering a single word, Archer stepped forward again until he was directly in front of me. I tried to back up but my back was against the wall.

Literally.

I couldn't help but flinch a little when he reached out to grab my left arm. I wasn't flinching because of him but because my shoulder still hurt like crazy and I didn't want him touching it. Still, I saw the brief look of guilt flicker across his face as he glanced up at me before he looked back down at my arm.

Gently, he began to roll up my sleeve. When I heard him take in a sharp breath, I glanced down at my arm and, sure enough, in the dim lighting, I could see the beginnings of a bruise forming where his hand had been.

That wasn't entirely his fault though. I bruised like a freaking peach.

After taking another deep breath, he rolled my sleeve back down and looked up at me and the guilt on his face was clear to see.

"I'm sorry I didn't mean—" I held my hand up, cutting him off.

"Just forget it. It's fine."

"No, it's not. I—"

"Archer, I said forget it. I'm fine."

73

"No. I didn't mean it. I would never do anything to hurt you on purpose. It's just that . . . you don't know what it's like being put in that situation and I don't like being constantly reminded of it. I just took my anger out on you and I—"

I cut him off for a second time, but this time, instead of words, I walked forward and wrapped my arms around him and pressed my head to his chest in what I hoped was a comforting hug.

I didn't give out too many of these, so he had better consider himself lucky.

I felt him tense before he slowly lifted his arms and wrapped them around me, returning the hug.

When I finally pulled back, I looked up at him and saw him already looking down at me with a confused expression on his face.

"What was that for?" he asked.

"That's me saying sorry. Again."

Archer frowned at that. "What do you have to be sorry for?"

I know now wasn't the greatest time to have another heart-to-heart about his horrible girlfriend and his backstabbing best friend, but he needed to hear it, and since our next thirty minutes of life weren't promised, I might as well tell him now.

"I didn't know you cared about her that much. I shouldn't have thrown it in your face like that. If it would've been the other way around and I was in your position, I probably would've done the same thing."

Archer shook his head and ran a hand through his hair, making it stick up at odd angles.

"That's no excuse though. I still shouldn't have taken it out on you."

"You're going through a lot right now. I couldn't imagine going through a seriously bad break-up, then being put in the middle of all of this, *and* having to deal with me," I said, gesturing around the tunnel. "So this one time, I'm letting you off the hook, but if you touch me again, I'll break all of your teeth."

The corner of Archer's mouth lifted in a small smile before he unexpectedly pulled me back into him and wrapped his arms around me in another hug. I felt my cheeks heat up as I wrapped my arms around him, and I was glad that it was dark enough so that he couldn't see me blush.

Again.

When he pulled away and looked down at me, he was smirking.

I cleared my throat nervously and looked away.

"Um yeah, we should probably get going."

Archer gestured ahead of him.

"Lead the way, Dora."

CHAPTER SIXTEEN

So it turned out that my navigating skills sucked a lot more than Archer's did, because I ended up leading us right back to the spot where we started.

"Nice," Archer commented as he surveyed our surroundings.

"Shut up," I mumbled as I turned in a circle, looking for another exit.

Just as I was about to randomly decide on which way to go and let luck do its thing, I saw a flurry of pink out of the corner of my eye. I turned to the left and stared straight ahead down the tunnel, trying to see if I noticed any movement.

Was I seeing things?

"Did you see that?" I asked Archer while still staring forward.

I heard Archer come up behind me. He was close enough that I could feel his breath tickling the back of my neck.

He really had no regard for personal space.

"See what?"

I continued to stare down the tunnel, squinting and un-squinting my eyes to try to see anything except for the empty tunnel.

Just as I was about to come to the conclusion that I was finally losing my mind down here, I saw the same flurry of pink dart across the tunnel and into another one.

"There!" I said, pointing.

Archer took a few steps forward and peered down the tunnel.

"What was that?"

I shrugged before a sudden guess to what or, better yet, *who* it was, hit me.

"The little girl! She was wearing pink, remember? That has to be her." I started forward, prepared to go after her but Archer grabbed my wrist, stopping me.

I looked over my shoulder at him and frowned. "What?"

"You do remember what happened not too long ago when you thought you were going after that little girl, right? We ran right into a trap and almost died."

I pulled my wrist back.

He did have a point.

"Yeah, but you just saw her."

Archer shook his head. "No, I saw pink. Anybody down here could be wearing pink, even one of those sick bastards just so they could try to trick us again."

I glanced over my shoulder and then back at Archer.

"Are you willing to live with the fact that *if* that was that little girl and we had the chance to try and save her, we didn't just because you *thought* that it wasn't her?"

"Are *you* willing to get yourself killed just because you thought that it *was*?" Archer shot back.

I groaned in frustration. "We don't have time for this. Look, I'm going to follow her. If you don't want to come, then fine. I won't force you but I'm going."

I turned on my heels and headed in the direction of where I saw the little girl. A few seconds later, I heard footsteps catching up with me. I smiled to myself, knowing that no matter how tough Archer appeared to be or how frustrating I was, he wouldn't leave me down here to fend for myself. Though when I glanced over my shoulder to look at him and give him a grateful smile, I was greeted with an entirely different picture.

I stopped dead in my tracks and turned all the way around.

Sheep Mask had one hand clasped tightly around Archer's arm and the other was clutching a knife, which was pressed directly against Archer's throat.

He tilted his head to the side, and I could practically hear the smile in his voice.

"You should've killed me when you had the chance, sweetheart."

CHAPTER SEVENTEEN

"You should've killed me when you had the chance, sweetheart," Sheep Mask sneered as he pressed the blade of his knife into Archer's throat. I could also see the gun that Archer had taken from him earlier tucked safely into the waistband of his jeans.

I watched as Archer winced and a small trickle of blood slowly made a trail down his neck.

I took a step towards him, but Sheep Mask only pressed the knife harder against Archer's throat.

"Ah, ah, ah. You take another step and your little boyfriend here will be looking like that old man."

I froze and stared with wide eyes at Sheep Mask as he continued to hold Archer at knife point.

"Now, here's how this is going to go. Dox is tired of chasing you, and he has made a special request for you, sweetheart. I'm here to deliver. If you don't cooperate, then your boyfriend is going to end up losing his head and we don't want that, do we?"

Sheep Mask took my silence as a yes as he shoved Archer forward, making sure he kept a firm grip on his arm and had the blade still pressed against his throat.

"Start walking."

I glanced at Archer once before turning and started to walk.

Sheep Mask led us down the same tunnel that I was sure the little girl ran through earlier, and I silently prayed that she was somewhere well hidden.

Once we reached the end of the tunnel, Sheep Mask stopped. With his left foot, he kicked open an old door with a sign that read, "Maintenance Only."

I was hesitant to walk inside the room. Sheep Mask seemed to notice my hesitation as he stepped forward and kicked me behind my knee. I stumbled forward and shot a glare over my shoulder.

"Move it," he snarled.

Before I turned around, I stole another glance at Archer and saw that his jaw and fists were clenched so tightly that his knuckles had turned white.

I silently prayed that he wouldn't try to do anything crazy.

I took a deep breath, trying to calm my racing heart before I took my first step into the room.

As soon as both of my feet were inside the room, the door slammed shut.

I heard Archer yell my name, and I spun around just in time to see his figure struggling against Sheep Mask through the small window on the door. I ran forward even though I knew it was too late. The door was closed and locked.

As I yanked on the doorknob in vain, Sheep Mask yelled, "Don't take this personally, sweetheart, but I had to get you out of the way! Dox doesn't want you. He wants your friend. Just be lucky I didn't kill you . . . yet."

His parting words, the sounds of shoes scuffling against the ground, and the low hum of the machines inside the room were the last things I heard before everything went quiet.

CHAPTER EIGHTEEN

ARCHER

Stunned, I watched as the door slammed shut, effectively cutting Gemma off from my sight. As soon as her face disappeared behind the door, I acted on impulse and rammed my elbow into Sheep Mask's face. He grunted from the impact, which caused him to loosen his grip on both my arm and throat.

Without thinking twice, I spun around and brought my fist forward and it connected with his face, mask and all. The force from the blow knocked his mask clean off his face, but I didn't have time to stand there and stare to see if he secretly looked like Freddy Krueger. Instead, I just ran into him shoulder first, sending us both to the ground.

To my disappointment, it turned out that Sheep Mask didn't look like Freddy Krueger at all. In fact, he looked like some random guy I'd pass on the street and not give a second glance. A mop of dark hair and eyes to match with a slightly crooked nose that suggested he had been in one too many fights.

A solid blow to my jaw brought my attention back to the man beneath me.

Dickhead. That's what I'd call him now since the mask was gone.

I looked down at him before bringing my fist down repeatedly on his face. He obviously didn't appreciate the new face

I was trying to give him because, soon after, he grunted and brought his head forward so it collided with mine.

People in the movies made it look easy. It felt like my brain was vibrating.

I groaned in pain. This gave him enough time to throw me off his body. He stood over me, and before I knew what was happening, he was ramming his foot into my ribs.

"You piece of shit! He should've asked for your little bitch in there. I'm sure she would've been a lot easier to handle," he sneered.

Anger flared through me. Before he could bring his foot down again, I grabbed it and twisted.

He actually screamed before he hit the ground.

With a grunt, I slowly got to my feet.

I stood over him, wiping the blood from the corner of my mouth with the back of my hand before tilting my head to the side.

"Who's a piece of shit now?"

When he didn't answer, I brought my foot down so that it rested on his throat and started to press down. His eyes went wide as he tried to remove my foot from his throat and clear his airway.

I bent forward and put one hand behind my ear.

"I can't hear you. Maybe you should try speaking a little louder."

When he still didn't answer, I pressed my foot down even harder, which caused him to start gagging and coughing. I released the pressure slightly and stared down at him.

"I'm waiting."

"I am . . ." he wheezed.

"You're what?" I knew I was playing with fire, but I couldn't help it or even bring myself to care. Especially not after he tried to kill me.

He struggled under my foot for a few more seconds before finally saying, "I'm a piece of shit."

A grin found its way to my mouth.

"Well, I'm glad you know."

And with that, I brought my foot down hard against his head, knocking him out.

I quickly reached down and grabbed the gun from his waistband and placed it in the back of my jeans.

I took a few deep breaths before turning around and heading to the same door that Gemma was locked behind. I walked up to it and placed my hands on the door, peering through the small window, but the window itself was made out of frosted glass so I couldn't really see her.

"Gemma, can you hear me?"

A few seconds later, a voice replied, "Archer, is that you?"

I sighed in relief before answering, "Yeah, it's me. Are you okay?"

"Yeah, I'm fine. I mean, I could use a shower and a burger right about now, but I can't complain, I guess."

I shook my head as a small smile tugged at my lips.

"Alright, I'm going to try and get you out."

I glanced down at the doorknob to take a look at the lock. Just as I was about to turn around and search Sheep Mask for the key, Gemma spoke again.

"Archer?"

Did she sound scared?

I pressed my ear up against the door and frowned. "Yeah?"

"Please hurry up and get this door open."

"Why? What's wrong?" I asked as panic started to surge its way through me.

"We really don't have time for twenty questions right now. Just get the door open!"

The fear and urgency in her voice got me moving. I quickly ran over to Sheep Mask and patted him down, searching his pockets. I sighed in relief as my hand closed around the small key. I quickly made my way back to the door and slid the key inside. To my relief, it unlocked easily, and I swung the door open. My relief was short lived though because as soon as the door was open, Gemma was nowhere to be found.

All that was left in the spot where she *should* have been standing was a small pool of blood instead.

CHAPTER NINETEEN

GEMMA

The hand that had a death grip on my hair was extremely close to pulling it all out, and I had to grit my teeth to keep from crying out or saying something that would get me killed.

Forget about trying to fight back. I quickly figured out that was a bad idea as soon as I saw Dox appear behind me through a connecting door to the room I was in with a flashlight and gun in his hands.

The bastard didn't even bother with the whole *'I've got you now!'* speech that most evil dudes say in the movies, which resulted in the victim having enough time to escape.

No, he just walked straight up to me, slammed my head against the wall and proceeded to drag me down a dark tunnel with blood now dripping from the back of my head like I was his own personal Raggedy Ann doll.

I had no idea where he was taking me, but I was in no hurry to get there. He obviously was though if the pace we were going at was anything to go by. He was practically sprinting.

We came to the end of the tunnel where it split off into two directions, left and right. He took the right one and then made two quick lefts and then another right. After his third left, I lost track of the way back just in case, by some miracle, I were to escape. It didn't seem like that was going to happen though. When he made yet another left, I spoke up.

"Where are you taking me?" I said through clenched teeth. He still hadn't loosened his grip on my hair.

"Shut your mouth or I'll snap your fucking neck," he snarled.

Grouchy.

His words had the desired effect though. I quit talking for about two seconds before I opened my mouth again. I was scared shitless, and when that happened, there was no shutting me up.

"Shouldn't you have killed me already? You said if you found any of us, we were as good as dead. Why won't you just go ahead and kill me now, get it over with." I don't know at which point my fear turned into anger, but it most certainly did.

Dox stopped abruptly and yanked my hair back, pulling me back into his chest. I let out a small whimper this time. I swear, I was going to have to start wearing wigs because of him.

When Dox leaned forward, I could feel his hot breath on my ear through the mouth hole in his mask.

"Now what fun would that be? Where's the creativity in that? Don't worry, doll. When I'm through with you, you'll wish that I would've just killed you." And with that, he started dragging me along again.

After another series of lefts and rights, we finally came to Dox's destination, and I almost pissed my pants for what I'm sure was now the tenth time today.

The room was large, made out of stone just like everything else down here and the ceiling and half of the walls were covered with pipes. In the center of the room stood four large curved gray pipes that jutted out from the floor and were pointed towards the right wall.

Handcuffed to three of those pipes and placed directly in front of them against the right wall were three people. The man who had tried to use me as bait earlier when this whole shit show started was handcuffed to the first one, except he looked a lot worse than when we had last seen him. They hadn't killed him, but they definitely did some damage. His face looked like it had been used as one of their punching bags.

The second pipe was occupied by the skater boy who had questioned Dox while we were all gathered on the tracks, and the person handcuffed to the last pipe . . . was the same little girl I had been trying to get to since I got down here.

Guess I got what I wanted.

"What the hell is this?!" I all but screamed.

Behind me, I could feel Dox chuckle, his chest vibrating against my back, before he spoke, "This is where all the fun happens."

He pushed me forward until I was standing in front of the only large pipe that wasn't occupied; it was only when I heard the small hiss of steam from one of the other many small pipes in the room that I finally realized what was happening and my heart dropped.

What I had originally thought were just large ordinary pipes were in fact, those big industrial steam pipes that let out buckets of blazing hot steam.

Now I understood why he had the other three people handcuffed in front of them.

I had stopped walking. Dox had to forcefully drag me forward in order to get me to move, but even then, I started to put up a fight. I did *not* want to be sitting in front of one of those things when that steam came out. It was going to sear us alive.

"No!" I tried kicking and clawing at Dox's exposed hands and wrists, even throwing my body left and right. Nothing worked, and when he slammed me up against the pipe that he intended to handcuff me to, I started crying. My body was trembling as Dox pulled out a pair of handcuffs from his back pocket and cuffed me to the pipe.

As soon as he stepped back, I turned my head so I could look at him through my watery eyes.

"W-why . . . why are you doing this?" I asked between my tears.

Dox patted the top of my head like I was some little kid.

"I already told you. The system already failed me once, and now, they're going to fail you. I'm proving a point."

"Then you make a fucking PowerPoint, get a laser pointer, and stand in front of a room full of people who actually give a shit about what you have to say!" I turned my head to see it was skater boy who had spoken.

When I turned back, Dox was shaking his head and slowly backing away towards the way we came from.

"I'd much rather give my audience a live show."

And with that, he disappeared back down the tunnel.

CHAPTER TWENTY

As soon as Dox was out of sight, I slumped against the pipe before sliding to the ground.

This was it. This was how I was going to die. Chained to a stupid pipe with a face full of blazing steam.

"This is such bullshit!" I lifted my head long enough to watch skater boy yank uselessly against the handcuffs before I dropped my head again.

"Are we . . . are we going to die?" a soft trembling voice asked from beside me.

I lifted my head and turned to the little girl next to me. There was no way I could tell her straight to her face that she was about to die, even if it was probably true.

I forced a smile and shook my head.

"Of course not. We're going to get out of here real soon," I lied straight through my teeth.

The little girl's bottom lip trembled, and I could see new tears forming in her big blue eyes. "That's what grandpa said, but that man hurt him anyway."

She started to cry and I had no idea what to do. There wasn't much I *could* do since I was handcuffed, but I hated watching other people cry.

"H-hey, don't cry. Everything is going to be fine, okay? How about you tell me your name, hmm? Mine is Gemma."

The girl sniffled loudly before she looked up at me again.

"Rose."

"Rose, that's a very pretty name. Just like the flower."

Rose smiled a little.

"Roses are my favorite. My mommy gives me one every year for my birthday," she said as she got a confused and faraway look on her face.

"Really? Well, I wish I had a pretty name like yours so I could get something nice like that for my birthday every year."

The girl focused back on me and her smile widened. "But your name is really pretty too. Gemma . . . it's like a . . . a . . . ." She bit her bottom lip as she did her best to think of something. "A gem! You can have your mommy give you a gem every year for your birthday!"

I smiled slightly and then suddenly had to fight back the new threat of tears that wanted to fall.

My mom.

I wondered what she was doing. *Did she know what happened? Were the police looking for us? Did Dad know?*

"Dylan."

I lifted my head, breaking myself from my thoughts and turned to the right to see skater boy staring at me.

"What?" I asked.

"My name, it's Dylan."

"Oh," was all I said. It's not like I asked him for his name.

Dylan turned to his right so he was now looking at the man who had tried to get me killed earlier. What good did it do now that we were both about to die?

"What about you?" Dylan asked him.

"What do you mean what about me?" he snapped.

"Your name? What is it?" Dylan urged.

"None of your damn business. We're all about to die and you're worried about names?!" the man yelled.

Rose instantly looked up at me with wide watery eyes again.

90

"I thought you said we weren't going to die? You said we were going to get out of here." Rose's bottom lip was trembling again.

"We are going—" I started to say but was cut off.

"She lied. You're going to die just like the rest of us, kid," the man cut in, and just like that, Rose was crying again.

"I don't wanna die," she mumbled as she sobbed.

"Rose, you're not going to die. I'll figure a way to get you out of here, okay?"

Rose ignored me completely and continued to cry.

I turned to glare at the man, who looked completely satisfied with himself, which only added to my anger.

"What the hell is wrong with you?" I demanded. "She's a little girl! Why would you tell her something like that?"

"This is the real world. The sooner she realizes that Superman and Prince Charming aren't going to come waltzing in to save her, the better."

I opened my mouth to reply but never got the chance to. The pipe in front of the man rumbled loudly and then all at once, the steam came rushing out.

*   *   *

ARCHER

This was such bullshit.

There was no way I was going to be able to find Gemma while also trying to find my way through all these tunnels. I had made so many lefts and rights, and I was completely lost now.

I ran my hands through my hair and had to resist the urge to punch the tunnel wall.

I was never going to find her, and that small pool of blood I found was doing nothing to reassure me that she was okay.

Just *as* I was about to turn around and try finding a different way, I heard a faint hissing sound quickly followed by a loud scream. Or maybe it was screams because it sounded like more than one person.

I blindly ran in the direction that I thought the screams were coming from. After making two quick lefts, I came to a large room filled with pipes, and there, sitting slumped forward, handcuffed, with her head down and trembling, was Gemma.

"Gemma!"

She whipped her head up at the sound of my voice. When she looked at me, I could see she had been crying.

I ran forward and bent down in front of her. I didn't hesitate to wrap my arms around her. She buried her head in my chest and I felt her body shake as she continued to cry.

"Archer, you have to get us out of here." Her voice was slightly muffled by my shirt.

When she pulled back, she had a wild and desperate look in her eyes.

"Don't let me die like this," she pleaded.

I had no idea what she was talking about until I looked over her shoulder. My eyes landed on the little girl Gemma had been trying to find first, then the guy with the piercing in his nose from earlier and then . . .

My eyes widened and I had to fight the urge to throw up. A figure, which had once been a person, was now just red—burned, bloody, and raw. The skin looked like it had been seared and melted clean off the bone in some places, and I could even see the white of their bones poking out in areas. I had to tear my eyes away once they traveled lower, and I could see that their skin had even melted against the handcuffs.

"What . . . what the hell happened?" I whispered as I looked back down at Gemma.

"The pipes. They shoot out hot steam, and he just got a face full of it. I don't know how much time we have before the next one goes off but you have to get us out of here."

I glanced down at the handcuffs and felt dread run through me.

How was I supposed to get her out of the handcuffs with no key?

I suddenly remembered the gun in the back of my jeans.

I quickly pulled it out and aimed it at the handcuffs.

Gemma pulled her hands as far apart as she could and shut her eyes tight before turning her head away and leaning back.

I aimed the gun at the chains, took a deep breath, and pulled the trigger.

There was a loud bang as the gun was fired, but when I looked down at the handcuffs, nothing had happened.

Gemma was still handcuffed to the pipes.

What kind of fucking handcuffs were these?

I quickly glanced around the room for anything else I could use and my eyes landed on the little girl. Or more specifically, her hair—she had two pink bobby pins in her hair.

I shot up and hurried over to her. When I knelt down next to her, I tried to give her a reassuring smile. She looked terrified.

"Hey. I'm going to get you out of here, okay? I just need to borrow one of your hair pins. Is that okay?"

The girl just looked up at me and nodded.

I gently took one of the pins out of her hair and was about to go back over to Gemma, but she shook her head.

"Get them out first," she said, gesturing toward the boy with the piercing and the little girl.

I glanced between them before looking back at Gemma.

"How do you know your pipe won't go off next?" I asked.

Gemma shook her head. "I don't, but if it's going down the line, then that means Dylan is next," she said as she looked down at the boy.

93

I gave her one last glance before I went over to the boy, who I now knew was named Dylan.

As soon as I was in front of him, he held his hand out as far as he could.

"Hurry, man. I do *not* want to end up like that."

I didn't have to ask him to know that he was referring to the charred remains of the person next to him.

I quickly inserted the pin in the keyhole of the cuffs and started to move it around. While I was concentrating on doing this, I heard a loud groan and then a rattling sound came from behind me.

I turned my head to the pipe directly behind me and knew instantly what was coming.

"Hurry!" Dylan yelled.

"I'm trying!" I said through clenched teeth.

The groaning and rattling grew louder. Dylan started to yank his hands against the cuffs.

"Stay still!" I yelled.

"Hurry the fuck up! Please, man!" Dylan kept yelling.

My hands were starting to sweat and I was having a hard time holding the pin steady. After having it slip a few times, I finally heard the audible click and the cuffs sprung open.

As soon as they were open, Dylan dived out of the way, knocking me over in the process as blazing hot steam poured from the pipe.

Even from a distance, I could feel the heat. When the steam subsided, I let out a sigh of relief. I glanced over at Dylan, who was still laying on his stomach on the ground, breathing heavily.

After wiping my hands on my jeans, I stood up and made my way over to the little girl.

Silently, she held her hands out, and I began the process of opening the handcuffs all over again. I had almost gotten them open when I heard the familiar groaning and rattling that let me know the steam was about to come.

I hurried and doubled my efforts to try and free the little girl. It was only when the noise grew louder that I noticed it—the sound wasn't coming from the pipe in front of the little girl.

It was coming from Gemma's.

I looked over at her, and our eyes met for a brief second before I got up and started fumbling with her handcuffs.

She stayed silent the whole time I was trying to unlock her handcuffs, but I could tell she was terrified from the way her hands kept shaking.

The next few seconds were a blur. At the same time that I heard the click that meant her handcuffs were now open was also when I heard the steam start to rush out of the pipe.

I grabbed Gemma's wrist and yanked her forward with so much force that we both fell to the ground. She landed on top of me with an *oomph* and I could feel her whole body trembling. She kept her head buried in my shirt and I let her stay that way.

I heard footsteps. When I looked up, I saw Dylan standing over me. Without saying anything, he bent down and took the pin out of my hand and went to free the little girl.

While he worked on her handcuffs, I felt Gemma lift her head off my chest. When I looked back down at her, she was staring back at me.

Without really thinking about it, I pushed a strand of her dark hair out of her face. I could see an angry red mark across her left cheek where some of the steam must have hit her. It wasn't too bad but it still made me feel bad; I should have moved faster.

I opened my mouth to tell her exactly that, but she shook her head and wrapped her arms around my neck and hugged me. It was kind of an awkward hug—with her laying on top of me and everything—but I wasn't one to complain so I wrapped my arms around her back and returned the hug as best I could.

I heard someone clear their throat above us. When I glanced up, I saw Dylan standing there with raised eyebrows. The little girl was standing next to him, and she obviously wasn't trying to hide her smile as she was smiling from ear to ear.

When Gemma lifted her head again and saw that we had a bit of an audience, her cheeks turned a slight shade of pink. She quickly scrambled to her feet. I stood up and dusted my jeans off.

"Umm . . . we should get moving," she mumbled.

"Do you know the way out?" Dylan asked.

I shrugged. "Not really."

"I guess we'll just have to walk until we find it then." Dylan started forward, followed by Gemma. I was about to follow when I felt a small hand grab mine. When I looked down, I saw the little girl looking up at me and smiling still. Her front tooth was missing.

"I knew it was true," she said.

I frowned. "What's true?"

The little girl glanced at Gemma and then back at me.

"Prince Charming does exist."

CHAPTER TWENTY-ONE

So apparently, my navigating skills were improving after all because I ended up getting us back to the entrance. Sure, I made a few wrong turns along the way, but the end result was the same.

I felt someone brush up against me as we were walking. I turned, fully expecting it to be Archer because, once again, that boy didn't understand the concept of personal space, but instead, I found Dylan standing next to me.

"So do you know where we're going or are we just taking in the scenery?" he asked.

For some unexplained reason, I glanced over my shoulder at Archer and saw Rose holding his hand while looking up at him with the widest smile on her face. I had no idea how she could be smiling at a time like this but I was glad to see it. It made sense that Archer, of all people, could make her smile after what she'd been through. I mean, who wouldn't smile while looking at a face like that?

Woah. Where the hell did that come from?

I quickly turned back around, ignoring the warmth spreading throughout my face from my thoughts, and I saw Dylan staring at me with a knowing look on his face.

"Why are you looking at me like that?"

Dylan shook his head, the look never leaving his face.

"I just asked you a question, but apparently, you were too busy getting an eyeful to notice." Dylan gestured to Archer with his head.

If it was even possible, my face became even hotter and I knew it probably looked like a beet now.

"W-what are you talking about?"

Dylan just shook his head.

"Don't play dumb. I saw what happened back there. I'd say you wanted to give him a lot more than just a simple thank you and a hug for saving you, if you know what I mean." Dylan wiggled his eyebrows.

My face was on fire.

"Give who a thank you?" I jumped at the sound of Archer's voice. When had he gotten so close?

I turned around and was now more aware than ever of how close we were.

"Um, I . . . h-he . . . ugh . . . what?"

Great job, Gemma. Way to show off your great speaking skills.

Dylan cleared his throat and when I looked back at him, he had one eyebrow raised, almost as if he was daring me to deny what he had just said.

I didn't have time for this. We had a bunch of psychotic masked lunatics running around and playing a game of extreme hide-and-seek. There was no time to talk about my love life—not that I had one.

"It's nothing. Let's just keep moving." I shot Dylan a pointed look before turning around and hurrying forward.

I was so busy trying to get away from Dylan and Archer and avoiding further embarrassment that I didn't even notice it. Not until it was too late.

The same time I heard Archer and Dylan scream my name was the same time I tripped over something and a black shadow darted out and struck me across the head.

Why the fuck did this keep happening to *me?!* Not that I wanted anything bad to happen to the others but there were other people down here too, dammit.

I had taken a statistics class, and while I didn't learn anything else from that unnecessarily difficult and pointless class, I knew that the probability that all of this stuff kept happening to me and me alone was extremely unlikely and yet . . .

It was like this entire place was out to get me.

I swear I had the luck of a black cat who lived under a ladder.

I felt pain shoot through my head from the impact as I hit the ground. My vision started to go in and out of focus, and I was vaguely aware of something swinging in front of me.

I groaned in pain and slowly rolled onto my side. It was just my luck that I happened to roll onto the side where I had dislocated my shoulder earlier. I sucked in a sharp breath and tried to ignore the pain and sit up.

Bad idea.

As soon as I tried to sit up, the tunnel seemed to tilt completely to the right and I fell back down with a thump.

I heard hurried footsteps before I felt someone touch my shoulder.

"Gemma! Gemma, are you okay?"

When my vision came back into focus, I saw Archer, Dylan, and Rose all hovering over me with worried expressions on their faces.

I tried to sit up a second time but Archer gently pushed me back down and said, "Don't move."

I groaned again. This was like *deja vu*. Wasn't I in this same position just a few hours ago?

I closed my eyes again and felt someone's fingers gently touching a spot on my head, which made me wince.

I opened my eyes and swatted the hand away.

"Stop that unless you want to lose your fingers," I muttered.

Archer shook his head, gave a relieved sigh, and just grinned at me while Dylan frowned. Rose still looked worried.

"What just happened?" I asked.

Dylan reached over me and grabbed something by my head. When he leaned back, he was holding a decent-sized rock in his hand.

My eyes widened in shock.

"Is that what hit me?"

Dylan nodded.

Archer leaned forward and tapped my forehead with his finger. "It's a good thing you have such a thick skull, huh? You've hit your head like ten times today."

"Shut up," I muttered. "How did that not bash my skull in?"

Archer smirked before answering. "You have serious hand, eye, and foot coordination. You actually tripped on the trip wire that set this off instead of stepping on it so the rock only clipped your head. If you weren't so damn clumsy, it probably would've been a lot worse."

"Thanks, you really know how to make a girl feel better," I said.

Note the sarcasm.

Archer just shrugged. "It's what I'm here for. Now," he said, gesturing to me with his hand. "Can you sit up?"

Before I could answer, Dylan had reached forward and slowly began to help me sit up. He put one hand on the small of my back and the other on my shoulder.

When I was sitting upright, the world still seemed to be spinning but not as much as it did just a few moments ago. I also noticed that Dylan still hadn't removed his hand on my back.

Out of the corner of my eye, I noticed Archer switching between looking at Dylan and at his hand on my back.

"Um, I think I can stand now," I said.

Both Dylan and Archer held their hands out to me at the same time.

I glanced between both of their hands, suddenly feeling very awkward.

This was just like in *Twilight* when Bella went to the movies with Mike and Jacob and both placed their arms on the armrests on either side of her seat, waiting for her to take their hands.

I glanced at their hands one more time before ignoring them both and pushing myself to my feet.

I swayed a little on my feet, and once again, Dylan was there placing one arm around my shoulder and the other on my arm.

I gave him a small smile. "Thanks, I'm fine." I took a small step away from him and cleared my throat.

"What do you think you're doing, mister?"

Everyone looked down at Rose, who had just spoken. She was looking up at Dylan with her arms crossed and an angry pout on her face.

Dylan frowned. "What are you talking about?"

Rose pointed her little finger at him accusingly. "You're not supposed to help Gemma; her Prince Charming should do that," she stated.

My what?

"Her what?" Dylan voiced my unasked question.

Rose huffed in annoyance.

"Her Prince Charming," she said again, but this time, she pointed at Archer. "He's supposed to help her, not you."

I glanced at Archer and saw that he was already looking at me with an unreadable expression on his face, then just like that, it was gone and replaced with his usual smirk.

He took a few steps forward until he was right in front of me. Then, without warning, he slipped his arm around my waist and pulled me close to his side, being careful not to bump my shoulder.

I stared up at him with a look that said, "What the hell are you doing?" He shot a smug look at Dylan, who didn't look too happy.

"You heard her. Only her *Prince Charming* is supposed to help, so why don't you go and find one of the ugly stepsisters?"

I couldn't help the small bit of laughter that came out of my mouth.

Dylan rolled his eyes and turned around. "Whatever," he mumbled before he walked forward again. Obviously satisfied with herself, Rose turned and followed after him.

I was about to do the same but Archer held me still.

I looked up at him with a frown. He waited until Dylan and Rose were a good distance away before he looked down at me and spoke, "Gemma, there's something I need to tell you."

The tone of his voice plus the feeling of his hand still on my waist wasn't doing my attention span any good. I could barely focus.

"Right now?" All I wanted to do right now was to try and find my way out of here as soon as possible.

Archer nodded. "With everything that's happening to us right now, I'm not sure if I'll get another chance to tell you, so I might as well do it now."

"W-what is it?"

Real smooth, Gemma. Real smooth. Keep stuttering.

Archer took a deep breath. "You remember when I said that there was—"

"Gemma, Archer! You need to come and see this!" Dylan's voice interrupted whatever Archer was about to say.

Archer glanced in the direction that Dylan and Rose went to before he sighed heavily. He took his hand from my hip and stepped away. I instantly missed his touch but I quickly shook that thought away. I shouldn't miss anything from him, especially not his touch.

Before Archer could walk away, I grabbed his wrist. Curiosity was going to kill me if I didn't know what he was going to say.

"Wait, what were you about to say?"

Archer shook his head.

"Doesn't matter." There was a pause. "We should probably go and see what they want." With that, he turned around and headed in the direction of Dylan and Rose.

After a minute, I followed him, still wondering what it was that he had wanted to tell me.

CHAPTER TWENTY-TWO

When Dylan had interrupted Archer and called us over, a small part of me was hoping that he'd found the way out of here.

No such luck.

Instead, I was greeted with what looked like freshly sprayed red paint across one of the tunnel walls.

Dylan and Rose were standing in front of it. Dylan had a look of confusion on his face while Rose was frowning like she was trying to figure out what she was looking at.

As we got closer, I realized that they were staring at words sprayed across the wall.

Dylan glanced at me over his shoulder, then back at the wall.

"What do you make of this?" he asked.

I stepped closer so I could get a better look and read the words out loud:

"It started out with two, looking for a door.
Because of bravery, there are now four.
One is the key to freedom and the other holds wisdom.
Let the wrong one lead you and you'll end up in a deadly prism.
Beware though, because all is not what it seems.
One in the group is the reason why you'll scream."

I read the words over and over again in my head before turning to look at Dylan and Archer.

"What kind of shitty poem is this?"

Dylan sighed and ran his hand through his hair.

Archer tilted his head to the side as he studied the words, then, as if he suddenly had it all figured out, he turned to us with a bright smile and wide eyes.

"You figured out what it means?" I asked eagerly.

Archer made a show of taking a deep breath and then all at once, his smile and wide eyes were replaced with a straight face as he answered, "No."

I narrowed my eyes at him before punching him in the shoulder.

"Ow! What was that for?!" he yelled while rubbing his shoulder.

"For being such an as—" I glanced at Rose quickly, then back at Archer. "For being such a butt," I amended.

Archer glanced at the words again then smirked when he looked back at me. "Well, I can make a few assumptions about the last part."

I watched as he stepped closer to me, then leaned in so his lips were just brushing up against my ear. I had to try really hard to control my breathing.

"I know a few ways to make you scream," he said, his voice low.

When he leaned back with that smirk still on his face, my face was burning.

I stared at him with wide eyes before I narrowed them at him again.

"You're supposed to be all heartbroken. Stop flirting with me," I huffed, then spun on my heels to study the words some more.

To my surprise, I heard Archer chuckle before I could feel him right behind me. "You could help me get over it a lot faster."

At first, I wasn't sure what he was talking about but when it hit me, my face heated up again.

Was this boy serious right now?

Once again, we were in a life-or-death situation, and here he was, thinking with that thing in his pants again.

"Why don't you go and bang your head against the wall and see if it'll make a hole big enough so we can get out of here?" I suggested.

Archer shook his head. "I'd rather bang something else."

Oh, my . . .

"Archer!"

Archer laughed and held his hands up defensively. "Okay, okay. I'm done."

I huffed and continued to study the wall. This really wasn't the time for this.

"Good, now put that big head of yours to use and help me figure this out."

"I'd rather use some other big part of my body to help you."

Before I could turn to punch him again, Archer had jumped out of my reach and was now on the other side of Dylan, who looked like he was trying his hardest to keep a straight face.

Dylan put his hand to his heart and shook his head. "It does my heart good when people can find love even in the worst situations. Being stuck in an abandoned subway tunnel with a bunch of asylum escapees trying to skin you alive always brings people closer. They should make a movie about this."

I shook my head and turned back to the wall, but not before shooting Archer one last glare.

"It started off with two, looking for a door," I mumbled to myself.

"That could mean you and Archer," Dylan pointed out. "You both started off together, right?"

I nodded slowly.

"Because of bravery, there are now four. That has to be about Archer. Because he saved you, me, and Rose, there's four of us now," I added.

106

"Okay, so what about the rest? Who's the key to freedom and who has wisdom?" Archer asked.

I shrugged. "I don't know, but I can make a safe bet and say that you aren't the one with wisdom," I said with a smirk.

Archer shot me a look. "Okay then, Ms. Wisdom, what's the deadly prism?"

I shrugged again. "I thought that was how you referred to shapes after you flunked geometry last year."

"I did *not* flunk. I got a fifty-nine point nine, which is basically a sixty, so I passed," he defended.

"Whatever helps you sleep at night," I shot back.

"You guys?" Rose spoke quietly.

"You're just mad because our geometry teacher was hot and had a thing for me." Archer continued grinning.

My eyes widened.

"You can't be serious."

"Umm, you guys?" Rose spoke again but I was barely paying attention.

"First of all, our teacher wasn't hot and she definitely didn't have a thing for you. She was married! The only reason you passed is because she didn't want to have to deal with you for another year."

"Oh, please, did you see the way she looked at me? I bet if I wanted, I could've had her bent over the—"

"I really don't want to hear about your gross imagination," I interrupted.

"They aren't imagina—"

"GUYS!!!"

Everybody stopped and turned to look at Rose. Her eyes were wide and her face a sickly pale color.

"What is it, Rose? What's wrong?" I asked.

Almost in slow motion, she lifted her arm and pointed ahead of her.

107

Everybody looked to where she was pointing, and my blood ran cold.

Standing at the end of the tunnel, completely silent and staring at us, was a man in a clown mask.

CHAPTER TWENTY-THREE

I needed a new bladder.

I was already close to peeing, and if stuff like this kept happening, my bladder was going to explode.

Everyone was silent and stood completely still as we stared at Clown Mask. He didn't move or say anything. He just stood there watching us.

I glanced towards my right, where the tunnel we had just come from was. We couldn't go back that way unless we wanted to end up completely lost and risk running into another one of Dox's friends or back in the room full of pipes, and I don't think anybody wanted that.

The only other way out was straight into the tunnel—right where Clown Mask just so happened to be standing in front of.

Great.

We continued our little stare down with Clown Mask until he slowly lifted his arm and pointed his leather-gloved finger straight ahead.

Right at Archer.

I glanced at Archer and saw that his face had gone completely pale. It was the first time he had shown any signs of real fear since we had been down here.

Clown Mask surprised everyone by moving his arm to the right and then pointed at someone else.

Me.

Lovely.

My heart just about burst out of my chest. This was the one time where I wouldn't mind not being chosen. Why couldn't it be like gym class where I was always picked last because I pretty much sucked at anything that involved running, throwing, catching, climbing, jumping, or things that made me sweat.

I continued to stare at Clown Mask, my heartbeat rapid, waiting for him to make a move.

"Screw it. I'll take my chances getting lost," I thought as I prepared to bolt out of there, but then I felt someone grab my hand, stopping me. I looked down and realized that it was Archer's hand. I glanced back up at him but he was still staring at Clown Mask. I felt him squeeze my hand in what was probably meant to be reassurance but it only added to my fear.

"What should we do?" I heard Dylan whisper next to me.

That was a good question.

What *should* we do?

Clown Mask obviously knew what he wanted to do next because suddenly, he started running towards us at full speed like he was a freaking track star.

I didn't know about everybody else but my fight or flight instinct kicked in and I sure as hell wasn't about to stay and fight. Everybody seemed to be thinking the same thing because at the same time, we all sprinted for the tunnel to our right.

I guess we were going to take our chances.

I was the first to reach the tunnel, and I didn't hesitate before running down the dim tunnel. I made a bunch of random lefts and rights, hoping that I didn't lead us to a dead end. The whole time I was running, Archer's hand never left mine. I wanted to look behind me to check if Dylan and Rose were okay or how far behind Clown Mask was but I didn't have the best coordination as it was—looking back was a disaster waiting to happen.

So I kept running.

Someone out there obviously cared enough about me because after the next right, we came upon another tunnel. As soon as we approached it though, we came across another problem. It went left and right.

"Which way?!" I asked frantically. I was bouncing up and down on my toes. I didn't like stopping, not when Clown Mask was probably right behind us.

"Right!"

"Left!"

Archer and Dylan spoke at the same time.

Dylan groaned. "We don't have time for this. We need to split up, it'll better our chances. Rose and I will go left, you and Archer go right."

I didn't have time to argue or tell Dylan that splitting up was probably the worst idea on the planet and that he obviously didn't watch enough horror movies because right after he spoke, we heard the heavy hurried footsteps of someone quickly approaching.

Three guesses on who it was.

With barely a glance back, Archer pulled me toward the right and we were running again.

The last thing I saw was Rose's pink coat before she disappeared with Dylan down the left tunnel.

CHAPTER TWENTY-FOUR

Now I kind of understood why the dumb people in the movies always seem to trip and fall flat on their faces when they were being chased.

Having to run for your life gives you a serious case of jelly legs.

As Archer pulled me down the tunnel, I had my fair share of trips and stumbles and it wasn't like I even had anything to trip over. I was just extremely clumsy and terrified. As a result, I kept tripping over my own feet.

If I got out of this alive, I'd never waste another good bowl of popcorn throwing it at the TV when the people in the movies always ended up falling.

As we continued to run, I tried to listen to see if I could hear any footsteps behind us that would mean that Clown Mask was following us. As much as I didn't want to hear his thundering footsteps behind us, in a way, I kind of did because if I didn't hear them, then that meant that he went after Rose and Dylan.

All of a sudden, I was jerked to the side and I stumbled, almost face planting the ground. When I righted myself, I looked up at Archer, ready to use every foul word I knew when he put a finger up to his lips, signaling for me to keep quiet, which only made me want to ask why. I was about to do just that when Archer pushed me up against the wall of the tunnel and into the shadows where the dim lighting didn't quite reach. When Archer pressed his body up against mine so that there wasn't an inch of space between us, I was close to panicking for a whole different reason.

What was he doing?

The feeling was quickly replaced with my earlier panic though as I heard booming footsteps. A few seconds later, I watched with wide eyes as Clown Mask went thundering past us and continued down the tunnel.

He hadn't seen us.

When I was sure that he was gone, I released a breath that I didn't realize I was holding, but that only lasted for about a millisecond before my breath hitched again, and I was having trouble swallowing.

Archer was still pressed up against me. He was so close that I knew he had to feel my rapid heartbeat. Or was that his?

I looked up at him and saw that he was already looking at me with that unreadable expression in his green eyes again.

How did we keep ending up in situations like this?

"Gemma."

Oh, my cheese balls.

His voice.

"I really need to tell you something, and I guess now is as good a time as any since I got interrupted last time."

I nodded and waited for him to continue.

Archer took a deep breath before he continued.

"Okay, so you remember how earlier when I said that there was another girl that I had feelings for before Avery but that she wouldn't give me the time of day?"

No way.

I'm pretty sure I was about to pass out. He couldn't be about to say what I thought he was about to say.

Now?

Here?

Right at this moment?

I nodded slowly.

Archer took another deep breath.

"Well—"

"Rose!" I suddenly called out.

Archer frowned at me.

"What?"

I pointed over his shoulder where Rose had just come into view, and even from here, I could see the red that stained her once pink coat.

Archer turned around. When he saw her, he pulled away from me, and we both hurried down the tunnel until we reached her.

I knelt down in front of her but kept my hands at my side. There was so much blood that I was afraid that I would hurt her if I touched her.

"Rose, where are you hurt?" I asked, frantically searching to see where the blood was coming from.

Rose shook her head. "I'm not hurt," she said, her voice trembling.

I frowned at that.

"Then why are you covered in blood?"

"Dylan," she answered. Rose only uttered one word, but that one word was enough to send chills down my spine.

No.

Rose looked at me with tears in her eyes. When she reached out and began to tug on my hand, I looked at her with a frown.

"Come on, hurry. He needs help," she said.

"You know where he is?" Archer asked as I got to my feet.

Rose nodded. "This way," she said and started to lead us down yet another tunnel.

She made a bunch of quick lefts and rights. It wasn't until we were back to where this whole thing started—on the train tracks in front of the old waiting platform—that I realized something was wrong.

There was no way Rose should have been able to know the way back. She made way too many turns for her to have memorized it by only going through it once.

I stopped walking at the same time as Archer. I turned to him and we shared a look.

He was thinking the same thing.

I watched as Rose climbed up on to the waiting platform and then turned to us.

A creepy little smile formed on her lips.

She turned to her left, and I guessed that she was looking at someone but I couldn't see who it was because of the subway train.

I watched in stunned silence as Dox suddenly came into view, picked Rose up, and placed her on his hip.

"Did I do good, Daddy?" she asked.

Daddy?

"You did great, sweetheart. Daddy's proud of you."

Rose smiled proudly.

Dox turned his head to the left and said, "Bring him out."

A few seconds later, Jason Mask and another man with a ski mask covering his face came out from behind the train, holding a bloody Dylan between them.

A gasp left my mouth, and I suddenly felt like I might pass out.

Dox turned back to me and Archer.

"Now that the whole gang's back together, we can pick up where we left off."

CHAPTER TWENTY-FIVE

I was still trying to process things.

This whole time, Rose was just playing us.

We got played by an eight-year-old girl.

Now that I thought about it though, things were starting to add up. Wherever we seemed to be, I'd always catch a glimpse of Rose right before Dox or one of his mental friends showed up. She was probably leading them to us the entire time, or maybe it was the other way around since we were now back to square one.

Then, there was the whole incident when we were chained in front of those pipes and Rose's didn't even go off. It skipped her completely and went straight to me. That was probably Dox's doing. There's no way he'd risk letting his little 'sweetheart' get hurt.

I could make a safe bet now and say that the old man that had been killed wasn't even her grandpa.

Since when did eight-year-olds become such good actors?

I had seen a few of the new kid shows that come on TV now, and she obviously hadn't gotten it from them.

"Finally putting it together, princess?"

I looked up at the sound of Dox's voice and took a small step back when I realized he was talking to me.

"Don't bother trying to run. You already had your chance. Now that you're here, I don't plan on letting you go again."

I had a really strong urge to tell Dox where he could put his plan, but I wisely kept my mouth shut.

"Honestly, I'm surprised you didn't figure it out earlier. I mean, I practically gave you the answer with that little riddle." Dox chuckled.

"I don't get it," Archer suddenly spoke up.

"Why send us off running when you were just going to lure us right back here, and why bother going through all that trouble when you could have just kept us here?"

"Well, that wasn't my original plan but since you and your little girlfriend decided to play Bonnie and Clyde with me earlier, I decided to give you both the special treatment."

"Lucky us," Archer muttered.

Dox placed Rose on the ground and clapped his hands together.

"Now, let's get this show on the road!"

Without warning, he pulled out the black handgun from earlier and jumped down from the platform so that he was now standing on the tracks with us.

Because my luck had been so great today—note my sarcasm—I ended up being closest to Dox and therefore, ended up having a gun pressed into my back.

"Walk," Dox ordered.

I didn't hesitate.

Dox led us around the back of the train and opened up the back exit. Once inside, Dox pushed me down on one of the seats and turned towards Archer, who had been glaring holes into the back of his head.

"Hold out your hands," he demanded.

Archer frowned. "Why?"

Dox shook his head and pointed the gun at my head, causing me to freeze up. "I don't have time for this. Hold out your damn hands or I'll put a bullet through her head."

Archer didn't hesitate this time. He held his hands out while Dox dug in his back pocket and pulled out a pair of handcuffs.

How many pairs of those things did he have?

I watched as Dox placed both of Archer's hands around one of the metal standing poles and handcuffed them around it. He then patted Archer down before reaching under his hoodie and grabbing the gun that Archer had placed there.

I was going to murder Archer, if Dox didn't do it first of course. He had a gun this entire time and hadn't used it when that creepy clown had been chasing us?

Dox spun around and stared at me through the holes in his mask.

"Don't move," he instructed before exiting the subway car.

He didn't have to worry. I wasn't going anywhere without Archer.

I looked up at Archer, ready to give him an earful about the gun only to find him already staring at me with an intense expression.

We just sat there staring at each other until he finally spoke, "I'm sorry."

I furrowed my eyebrows in confusion. What did he have to be sorry for?

"For what?"

"I promised you we'd get out of here, and now, look where we are."

I shrugged and tried to give him a small smile. "Well, if I'm being honest, I didn't think you'd get us as far as you did. So you get an A for effort."

Archer stared at me with a blank expression before a small smile broke out on his lips.

I couldn't help but notice how when Archer smiled, he looked so much better. I mean, don't get me wrong, he looked good anyway, but when he smiled, he looked even better.

Dear Lord.

I was losing my mind. All this crap was making me delirious.

"Gemma."

Archer's voice broke me from my thoughts.

"Yeah?"

"Come here."

I frowned and asked, "Why?"

"Well, I can't exactly go to you now, can I?" he replied sarcastically.

I rolled my eyes and stood up and walked over to him.

"Closer."

My heartbeat started to tap dance in my chest as I took the smallest possible step forward.

Archer sighed and shook his head.

"Closer."

"How much closer do I need to be?" I asked, my voice coming out high and squeaky.

"Closer than that. Stand right here."

I looked at the spot Archer had just gestured to in disbelief.

"I-I'm not standing there," I stammered.

He wanted me to stand in the *extremely* small place between his arms and the pole. Because his hands were cuffed to each side of the pole and the space between him and the pole wasn't big at all, it'd be almost like he was hugging me if I stood there.

"Come on, Gemma. Do this for me. It's important."

"Archer," I groaned.

"Please?"

All my earlier statements flew straight out the window.

I sighed and took another step forward before ducking under one of his arms and standing back up. I was now officially enclosed in his arms.

The lack of space between us was definitely noticeable.

I swallowed nervously and looked everywhere but at him.

"Gemma."

Why did he have to sound like that?

Slowly, I looked up at him and my breath was caught in my throat. He was looking at me with that intense expression again but there was something else there.

"Yeah?" I answered my voice barely above a whisper.

After a moment's hesitation, he spoke, "It was you. Even before Avery."

If the pole and Archer's arms weren't there, I probably would have hit the floor.

He couldn't have said what I thought he just said.

Could he?

"W-what?" I squeaked.

"The girl I told you about earlier—the one I had feelings for. It's you. I know the timing is shit, because we're most likely dead anyway, but I needed you to know."

My head was spinning. There was no way that Archer Daniels could have feelings for me.

I shook my head. "No, you don't. You can't."

Archer pressed his body up against mine, getting rid of the small space that *had* been between us. "And why not? I'm pretty sure I know how I feel."

I couldn't form a single coherent thought, let alone a sentence. The only thing I could focus on was his body pressed up against mine.

"You just can't."

I wanted to slam my head against the pole.

"But I do. So now what?" he asked, tilting his head to the side slightly.

Now what?! I was still trying to process the part where he said he had feelings for me and he wanted to know 'Now what?'

"I, um . . . I don't know . . . I . . . guess." Was that even a sentence?

That small smile that had been on his lips earlier reappeared.

Hmm. His lips.

Why was I suddenly thinking about his lips?

Abort mission!

I needed to go back and sit down.

Fast.

I was about to do just that and pretend that Archer Daniels hadn't just declared he had feelings for me when he leaned down and pressed his forehead against mine.

"I really want to do something, and this may be the last chance I get to do it. Will you let me?" he asked, his voice was still low.

Jesus Christ.

"What is it?" Look at that. A sentence.

"Let me kiss you."

CHAPTER TWENTY-SIX

Did he just ask me that?

Did he use to be a freaking member of One Direction or something?

He couldn't have just asked me if he could kiss me. Especially now of all times.

As I stood there, thinking the same thing over and over again, I realized Archer was staring at me.

He was waiting for an answer, so I took a deep breath and gave him one.

"You do realize that the couple who makes out in horror movies always end up dead, right?"

Archer let out a short laugh and a mischievous grin formed on his lips.

"So you consider us a couple after just one day, huh? You like to move fast, don't you?" he said with that stupid little smirk still on his face.

I rolled my eyes at him.

"Did you really just ask me that?" I shook my head when Archer opened his mouth to answer. "Never mind, don't answer that. Look, there's something you should probably know that—" I hesitated, thinking about what I was just about to say and then decided against it.

I'd rather take it to my grave.

"Never mind."

Archer frowned at that. "Don't do that. I hate when people do that. What were you about to say?"

I shook my head and looked anywhere but at him. "Nothing."

"Gemma."

"Archer," I said, copying his tone but still not looking at him.

"What were you about to say?" he repeated but this time slower, like I had a hard time understanding him the first time.

I huffed in annoyance.

"Ihaven'tkissedanybodybefore," I mumbled quickly.

"What?"

I groaned in frustration.

"I said, I haven't kissed anybody before. There, are you happy now? Would you like for me to say it a little louder so everyone can hear?"

There was no way I was going to look at him now.

I'd be turning nineteen next year, *if* I survived this little shebang that is, and I *still* hadn't had my first kiss. I only had one boyfriend before and sure, I kissed him, but it was only a brief peck on the lips or cheek. He who shall not be named, wanted to take it a lot further than what I was ready for, and I ended up breaking up with him before things got too carried away between us.

Archer was probably rethinking the whole let-me-kiss-you thing now. I couldn't say that I really blamed him either.

"Gemma, look at me," Archer said.

I shook my head. "Why? So you can laugh in my face? No thanks."

"I'd never laugh at you . . . well, I probably would but not about this."

I couldn't help the small smile that formed on my lips.

"Can't you take anything seriously?" I asked, finally gaining the courage to look at him. "We're literally knocking on death's door here."

Archer smirked and shrugged.

"Sure I can, when the situation calls for it."

"And this situation doesn't call for it?" I asked.

Archer pretended to be in deep thought for a few seconds before shaking his head. "No, I can't say that it does."

"You're impossible," I said through a small nervous laugh.

"Quit trying to change the subject. So you've never kissed anyone at all? Boy? Girl? Dog? Pillow?"

I shot him a look before answering.

"No, I haven't."

"Well, we're going to have to fix that." His voice had taken on that low tone again that had my heart ready to leap out of my chest.

"But first things first . . ." I frowned at Archer as he began to move his hands around and the handcuffs kept clanking against the metal pole.

"What are—"

Before I could finish asking him what he was doing, Archer held his hands up. I stared in shock as the handcuffs hung loosely from his finger.

"How did you do that?" I asked, still staring at the handcuffs.

Archer waved a little pink bobby pin in front of my face.

"I took this back from Dylan before we split up."

"Huh, who knew you had it in you to actually use that tiny brain of yours," I teased.

Archer rolled his eyes, then shoved the bobby pin back in his pocket.

"Ha-Ha. You're hilarious. Now, I'm pretty sure we have unfinished business," he said as he stepped closer, eliminating the small space that had been created between us while he was undoing his handcuffs.

"Um . . . I'm pretty sure it can wait," I said, smiling nervously and trying to step around him. "We should try to go and

124

get Dylan and get out of here." Before I could take another step, Archer had grabbed my wrist and pulled me back to him.

"I don't care if the fucking world is ending. If this is my last and only chance to kiss you, then I'm going to take advantage of it."

I swallowed hard, my mouth suddenly dry.

"Well, who says I want to kiss you anyway?" I asked.

Who was I kidding? Archer and I both knew that I wanted to kiss him right now.

Yes, I admit it, go ahead and sign my name to the list. I admit defeat. I couldn't help it.

Might as well hang my head in shame.

"So you're saying you *don't* want to kiss me?" he asked.

My breath caught in my throat as he tucked a stray strand of hair behind my ear and then let his hand linger on my cheek.

"N-no?" I said, but it came out as more of a question.

"I think you're lying."

"I'm not."

"Prove it."

"How am I supposed—" But before I could finish my sentence, Archer had leaned in and pressed his lips against mine.

My eyes widened in shock and my thoughts were along the lines of "*Oh, my gosh! Archer Daniels is kissing me! Ha! Suck it, Avery!*" and "*Sure, we're probably about to be turned into human shish kebabs at any moment, but screw it.*"

My eyes soon fluttered close, and I let myself completely forget about our current situation. You know, the one where we were probably about to die at the hands of a maniac.

I reached up and wrapped one arm around his neck, pulling him closer and using the other to run my fingers through his hair. He made a sound at the back of his throat that sounded like a cross between a moan and a groan. Either way, it had me wanting to turn into a puddle.

125

The way his lips moved against mine was literally otherworldly, and when he traced my bottom lip with his tongue, I had a small heart attack. Keep in mind, this was my first kiss. I had no idea what I was doing so I just kind of went with the flow and prayed that I didn't end up biting him.

When his hands gripped my hips, pulling me against him, I knew I had to at least be doing *something* right. When his tongue entered my mouth, I'm pretty sure fireworks exploded in my mouth. It was either that or he had eaten pop rocks.

When I finally pulled away, not because I wanted to, but because my stupid lungs needed air, we were both breathing hard. I'm pretty sure most of it had nothing to do with the fact that we actually needed air.

Archer rested his forehead against mine for a second and closed his eyes.

"So that happened," I whispered to myself.

"Hmm," Archer hummed, opening his eyes again.

"So how was that for your first kiss?" he asked.

What was that?

Did I detect a hint of nervousness in his voice?

"Unforgettable," I breathed out. I was beginning to understand more and more why girls fell at this guy's feet. His kisses were the equivalent of finding extra French fries at the bottom of your bag.

Romantic, I know.

"Unforgettable good or unforgettable bad?" He still actually looked a little nervous.

I smiled up at him. "Despite the circumstances, definitely good."

Relief washed over his face. "Good. Because I plan on doing it a lot more from now on."

Before I could say anything, Archer grabbed my hand and started dragging me toward the subway car exit, but as soon as we reached it, the door slid shut.

Archer frowned and let go of my hand so he could try and forcefully push the door open.

It didn't work.

Archer hurried over to the side exit and got the same result.

My heart was starting to race again.

We were trapped.

All of a sudden, the doors that connected and led to the other riding cars opened all at once, and I was able to see straight down—all the way to the front of the train.

What I saw made my stomach drop.

"Archer, look," I said, my voice small.

Archer turned around with a frown as he looked at me, probably wondering why I sounded the way I did, then his eyes followed my gaze to the front of the train. I could see the color drain from his face.

"Shit."

The subway train was on fire and the flames were quickly making their way towards the back.

Towards us.

CHAPTER TWENTY-SEVEN

I watched as the flames crept their way up the walls and across the floor of the subway car, slowly inching their way towards us.

I could already smell the smoke as it started to fill and burn my lungs.

I turned towards Archer with wide eyes, hoping he'd know what to do because I sure as hell didn't. However, when I looked at him, my heart dropped. He looked just as panicked as me. When our eyes locked and he gave me a slight shake of his head, I knew we were screwed.

He had no plan. We were stuck, and in just a few moments, we were going to be consumed by the flames.

Because I didn't have a better plan and I refused to just sit here and burn, I ran back to the exit door and began pushing, pulling, and even banging on the door.

Nothing worked.

As the flames of the fire slowly crept their way closer, the smoke got thicker and a few harsh coughs came from my throat. I pulled the collar of my shirt up over my mouth and nose, trying to block out some of the smoke.

I glanced back over my shoulder and my heart dropped. The fire was halfway towards us. Only a few more minutes and we'd have nowhere left to run to.

Panicking, I started banging on the small glass window of the exit door with my fists until my fists turned red and sore. When that didn't work, I let out a frustrated scream and kicked the door before slumping to the ground on my hands and knees.

The smoke had gotten a lot thicker in what seemed like only a few seconds and my lungs started to feel like they were being barbecued. My eyes were burning, and I was having trouble seeing straight.

I felt a hand on my shoulder, and when I looked to my left, I saw Archer kneeling next to me. It looked like he had ash smeared in places all over his face. Without saying anything, he lifted me up by my shoulders so I was standing again.

"If we can break that glass, then we can climb out," Archer said, gesturing toward the exit window.

I looked at the window and then down at my hands, which were still red and hurting from when I had tried banging against it earlier.

"Not sure how much help I'll be with that," I said after a few coughs.

The fire had devoured the last subway car before ours and was just starting to consume the one we were in. If we didn't break this window in the next few minutes, we were dead.

"On three, kick the glass, okay?" Archer said.

I nodded and turned towards the window.

"One."

"Two."

"Three!"

We kicked the window at the same time, and I put as much force as I could into that kick. To my relief, the window actually cracked.

"Again!" Archer yelled.

He didn't bother counting this time. Instead, he just kicked the window when I did.

The cracks in the window grew but unfortunately, so did the fire. I could feel the heat from it on my back. Sweat and ash were now covering my face and hair.

"Now!" Arched yelled and we kicked the window again.

I almost screamed in relief when the glass gave and shards of it fell out and onto the tracks.

Archer didn't waste any time and quickly took off his black hoodie, leaving him in just a gray t-shirt.

He placed his hoodie over the sill of the window so that it covered the few pieces of glass that were still sticking up and reached his hand out for me to take.

I took his hand and let him help me out the window. I swung one leg over and held on to the windowsill with one hand while still gripping Archer's hand with the other. I pulled my other leg through, and when Archer let go of my hand, I fell in an ungraceful heap on the tracks, banging my knees painfully on the tracks.

A few seconds later, I heard a grunt and turned to see Archer on his hands and knees next to me.

I sighed but then winced at the burning sensation that was still lingering in my lungs.

"You okay?" I heard Archer ask as I slowly rolled onto my back.

"No. I'm pretty sure my knees are going to be bruised for life, my lungs feel like they've been baked, my body hurts just about everywhere, and I'm covered in sweat, ash, and blood."

To my surprise, Archer actually laughed.

I would've said something, but I didn't even have the energy anymore. Instead, I just shook my head and closed my eyes. I could see the brightness from the fire behind my eyelids but then, it was suddenly dimmed. I opened my eyes slowly to see Archer hovering over me and staring at me intently.

"What?" I asked. "Do I have something on my face? I mean, besides the sweat, ash, and blood?"

Archer smiled and shook his head.

"You're the only girl I know who can make blood and sweat look sexy."

Cringe.

Still, I gave a nervous laugh, trying to ignore the warmth in my cheeks and sat up slowly. I took Archer's hand when he offered and let him help me up.

When I was on my feet, I looked up at the burning subway train and watched as the flames of the fire completely engulfed it.

"What do we do now?" I asked quietly.

"We get the hell out of here," Archer said with a determined glint in his eyes.

"What about Dylan? We can't just leave him here."

Archer glanced down the tunnel then back up at the old platform before sighing heavily.

"Is there anything I could say to you that would make you leave while I stayed and got Dylan?"

I crossed my arms over my chest and narrowed my eyes at him.

Archer sighed again. "I didn't think so."

It would've been easy. If I kept going straight down this tunnel, I would eventually come to a waiting platform that was in use where people would be and I could get help and escape, but there was no way I was leaving Archer down here by himself with Dox and his twisted friends.

I grabbed Archer's hand and stared him straight in the eyes.

"Wherever you go, I go. You can't get rid of me that easily, and if that's what you're trying to do, then you're going to have to try a lot harder."

Archer stared at me for a moment before leaning in and quickly kissed me.

Okay, so we were doing this more frequently then.

When he pulled away, he had a small smile on his lips.

"Let's go then," he said, tugging on my hand.

131

"Where are we going?"

"To get Dylan."

CHAPTER TWENTY-EIGHT

So it turned out that Dox decided to stick around and watch after he tried to turn me and Archer into human bits of charcoal.

We were crouched down by the back of the still burning subway train, looking up at the platform where Dox stood. He was holding Rose's hand as he stared at the flames. The fire cast bright reds, yellows, and oranges across his flesh-colored mask, making him look ten times creepier.

Looking at him now, I was close to saying screw Dylan and running for my life and letting the police deal with it.

Unfortunately, I *did* have a conscience and it didn't like the idea of leaving Dylan, so I stayed put.

I tore my eyes away from Dox and the little she-devil that was apparently his daughter and searched the platform for Dylan. I found him sitting slumped against the wall, his head hanging low between his knees. Jason and Ski Mask were standing guard on either side of him.

I leaned back and turned to Archer.

"What do we do now?" I whispered. No one should be able to hear us over the sounds of the fire. If they didn't hear us smashing the glass to get out of the subway car, then I doubt that they could hear us talk, but I didn't want to take any chances.

"I'll go up there and play rock, paper, scissors with him for Dylan. Best two out of three."

I groaned and put my head in my hands.

I felt Archer pat my back. "I'm sure if we ask nicely, he'll let you play too."

"We're so screwed," I mumbled into my hands.

"No, we aren't. I'll have you know that I haven't lost a game of rock, paper, scissors since I was in the fourth grade."

I wanted to scream.

I turned to Archer and spoke *very* slowly as if I were talking to an eight-year-old child—one who wasn't a possible descendant of the devil himself like that pink she-devil.

"Archer, listen to me carefully, okay? We are *not* playing rock, paper, scissors for Dylan. Your idea sucks ass."

"No please, tell me how you *really* feel," Archer said, his voice drowning in sarcasm.

"I'm serious. We need a plan that isn't going to get us all killed."

"Well, since you don't like my idea, come up with something better."

And just like that, I had an idea.

"I got it. I know how we can get Dylan."

Archer raised that one eyebrow like all guys seemed to be able to do and I couldn't.

"Trust me, this'll work."

I hope.

*   *   *

I took a deep breath, trying to calm my racing heart as I prepared myself.

I glanced behind me one last time before I took the few steps forward so that the burning subway train was no longer hiding me. I quickly crawled up onto the waiting platform. When I saw Dox's fleshy mask turn towards me, I almost turned around and hauled ass the other way. However, instead of running *away* from him, I ran towards him while screaming like a maniac. I even had my arms outstretched like I wanted to choke the life out of him—which I did.

"You bastard! You killed him!" I yelled as I slammed my body into Dox's.

I forced tears into my eyes, which wasn't that hard with all the smoke in the air and the brightness of the fire.

"You killed him!" I screamed again, and this time, I tried clawing at any piece of exposed skin I could get to.

Dox, who was obviously shocked by both the fact that I wasn't dead and my little outburst, seemed to snap out of it as he grabbed me roughly by my wrists and squeezed them tightly.

Please don't let him kill me now. That was not a part of my plan.

"You sick bastard! This is all your fault! You killed him! He's dead!" I let a few tears fall and gave what I hoped was a believable sob.

The gears must have started to turn because I heard Dox chuckle darkly.

"Did he not make it out of the fire?"

I tried to claw at him again but Dox clamped down on my wrists tighter.

"I don't even know how *you* made it out alive," he said, cocking his head to the side, like he was trying to figure out how I could've possibly made it out while Archer didn't.

"Burn in hell," I spat.

"You mean like how your boyfriend burned in that fire?"

Dox suddenly laughed loudly.

"This is just too good! I didn't expect this, but I'm always up for a change in plans. You and I can have some fun now. What do you say?"

Dox yanked me closer so that my body was pressed against his. He leaned forward so that the mouth hole in his mask was next to my ear.

"I don't know about you, but I plan to have a lot of fun with you," he whispered.

I struggled and tried to push myself away, but he just tightened his grip.

"You see, sweetheart, this just proves my point. You're going to go through hell and there is *no one* here to save you. No boyfriend, no police, no one. You're all alone."

An involuntary shiver ran down my spine.

"Tell me, how do you feel knowing that no one can help you? That no one can save you?" Dox whispered.

I quickly glanced over Dox's shoulder, then focused my eyes downward and let a small smile spread across my lips.

"The real question is, how do *you* feel about it?" I asked.

I felt Dox tense before he pulled back so he could look at my face.

"What are—"

Dox never got to finish his sentence as a shard of glass was pushed straight into the center of his back.

Dox gasped and let go of me before stumbling backwards.

"You . . . you . . ." Dox stammered.

I shook my head and gave him an innocent look.

"I didn't do it."

Dox spun around slowly, swaying on his feet to face the person who had stabbed him in the back.

Literally.

"Hi." Archer waved.

"You little bastard. I'll kill—"

Dox's sentence was cut off yet again as Archer drove the glass into him again, but this time straight into his chest.

I watched as Dox turned his head, probably looking for his two other psychotic buddies to come and help him, or maybe even his little spawn of Satan, but no one came.

"Kind of sucks having no one to help you, doesn't it?" Archer asked angrily.

"How does it feel to die all alone?" Archer asked in a low voice just as Dox gave one sharp gasp for breath and then slumped to the ground.

CHAPTER TWENTY-NINE

I stared at Dox's motionless body. With our bad luck, I kept expecting him to pop back up at any minute and yell, "Surprise! I'm not really dead!"

However, nothing happened.

I looked at Archer, who was also looking at Dox with an apprehensive look on his face.

I had the urge to nudge his body with my foot to see if he moved at all but decided against it.

"So this is it, right?" I asked. "He's dead. We can leave now."

"I hope you weren't planning on leaving without me."

I jumped at the sound of the new voice and looked past Archer to see Dylan standing there with his arms crossed.

It was kind of odd seeing him standing there like that. He was still covered in blood and looked like he had just woken up from a nap with death.

Archer practically spoke my thoughts out loud when he suddenly said, "What the hell are you doing up? You're supposed to be over there dying." Realizing how that sounded, he quickly added, "Not that I want you dead or anything."

Dylan shook his head. "Why am I having a hard time believing that?"

Archer shrugged.

"How are you even up and walking? The last time we saw you, you couldn't even stand up on your own," I questioned.

"It's called good acting," Dylan stated simply.

"So why didn't you help me take out Thing One and Thing Two?!" Archer demanded, wildly gesturing to his right.

It was only then that I noticed two other bodies lying on the ground where Dylan had once been sitting.

Jason and Ski Mask.

I glanced back at Archer.

"Y-you killed them too?" I asked quietly.

Archer studied my face intently for a while before he nodded once.

I swallowed the lump in my throat before nodding myself.

I guess that *had* been a part of my plan. While I distracted Dox, Archer grabbed a piece of glass from the broken window of the subway car and snuck around the other side. While Dox was busy giving his celebratory "I've beat you" speech, Archer took care of Jason and Ski Mask. Knowing that he had the glass, I guess I really hadn't expected him to just go up and prick their fingers but it was still hard to swallow.

Then another thought popped into my head.

"Archer?"

"Yeah?"

"Where's Rose?"

Archer gave me a sheepish grin and took a few steps back. Sitting a few feet behind us was Rose with some type of black cloth stuffed into her mouth and handcuffs on her wrists.

"Really, Archer? You handcuffed *and* gagged her? She's eight," I said, shaking my head.

"She's a *conniving* eight-year-old though. Plus, she tried to bite me," he added while rubbing his right hand. "I *had* to gag her."

I sighed and walked over to her. I leaned down and carefully removed the gag and, almost instantly, she started screaming.

I jumped back and covered my ears.

She screamed like a banshee.

I hurried forward and quickly placed the cloth back in her mouth.

"Archer, really? She's *eight*." I heard Archer's voice as he mocked me.

I shot him a look.

"Anyway, how did you manage to take care of those two?" I gestured to both motionless bodies. "And Rose without getting caught?"

"I'm part ninja," Archer said with a serious face.

I just shook my head.

"Can we get out of here now?" Dylan asked.

"What about everybody else? They're still wandering around in the tunnels," I pointed out.

"Oooh no, we're getting the hell out of here and letting the police do their jobs. Let's go." Archer started pushing me towards the set of old steps that should lead us up and out of the subway station.

"Aren't you forgetting something?" Dylan called out.

Archer stopped and turned around.

Dylan pointed at Rose.

Archer grimaced. "You grab her. She obviously doesn't like me. I don't know why because *everybody* likes me."

"I don't," Dylan said.

"I said, *everybody* likes me," Archer repeated.

"Yeah, and I said, I don't."

"Exactly, because you're a *nobody*. Now, grab the little pink beast and let's go."

Archer started pushing me towards the steps again. Dylan grunted before picking up a struggling Rose and throwing her over his shoulder.

Together, we managed to make it up the stairs using the light of Archer's cell phone.

140

When we made it to the top of the stairs, we came across what felt like the hundredth problem of the day.

The exit was boarded up.

CHAPTER THIRTY

"You've got to be kidding me!" Archer yelled in frustration.

"It's not possible for someone to have *this* much bad luck. This has got to be against some kind of law somewhere," Archer continued to vent and kicked the wall. "I can't believe this."

"I can," Dylan scoffed.

I turned to look at him with a frown.

"What are you talking about?"

Dylan gave me a hard look before saying, "You two. Wherever you go, something bad happens, so this shouldn't be a surprise."

Archer quit his angry mumbling now to turn and look at Dylan, who still had a struggling Rose thrown over his shoulder.

"What are you trying to say?"

Dylan sat Rose down on the ground. She sent him a glare as she fell on her butt, but he barely noticed her. He was too busy glaring at Archer and me.

He took a threatening step forward and pointed his finger in my face.

"You two are nothing but trouble. First, I get the bad luck to be chained to a pipe, waiting for a face full of steam, and who does that masked creep drag in? You!" he yelled as he stared at me with hateful eyes.

"Then I follow you guys around, hoping that maybe you guys could help me make it out of here in one piece, and where do you lead me? To *another* one of those creeps!"

In the dim light from Archer's cell phone, I could see Dylan's face turning a dark shade of red.

"Then we get split up and guess who gets caught? I do! And where were you two, huh? Where the hell were you two? Now, we're here looking for a way out and what happens? It's blocked!" Dylan is practically screaming now.

Archer reached out and pushed me a few steps back.

"You can't seriously be trying to blame that on us when there were five mentally challenged nutcases running around and trying to kill us. No one told you to split up, that was *your* idea, and no one told you to follow us either! You did all of that on your own. Now, you're trying to pin it on us?! If anything, you should be thanking us. We saved your ass. *Twice,* if I remember correctly. In fact, if it wasn't for Gemma, you would've still been down here because she's the one who wanted to come back for you. I would've left your sorry ass down here."

Dylan took one more step forward so he was right in Archer's face.

"You know what? You're right. I don't blame her. I blame you." A nasty smirk was now plastered on Dylan's face.

Where the hell was all this even coming from?

He either had a serious case of bipolar disorder or I was really bad at reading the signs.

"I think that this whole time, you were just trying to get rid of me."

"Get rid of you? What the hell are you talking about?" Archer demanded. "We just saved you!"

"You see me as a challenge, don't you?" Dylan asked.

Yep. He had lost his fucking mind.

Dylan didn't give Archer a chance to answer, he just kept rambling, "You wanted me out of the way because you didn't want

143

me near her." Dylan pointed at me. "That's why you want me dead, isn't it? What, you scared I'll take her from you or something?"

"Dylan, this is not the time—" I started but he cut me off.

"Oh, it's the perfect time. I want you to answer this question for me, Gemma. Don't you find it even the slightest bit odd that he can kill so easily?"

"What?" I asked quietly.

"Lover boy here. Don't you find it odd that he can kill another human being without batting an eye? How many people has he killed down here? Two? Three? And does he even look the littlest bit affected by it?"

"I did what I had to do so we could survive, otherwise we'd be dead," Archer said through clenched teeth.

"How do we know that?" Dylan asked.

"You just killed three people. Three people whose blood is now on your hands. Now tell me, Gemma, does the thought of him trying to kill one more person sound that odd to you now?"

For some reason, the memory of Archer getting ready to kill the guy in the Sheep mask came to mind. How Archer was so willing and ready to kill him. If I hadn't said something, he would've killed him too.

Yeah, and if he had killed him, you guys could've been out of here by now.

The little voice in the back of my head had a point. However—even though I hated to admit it—so did Dylan. I didn't want to doubt Archer, but he *was* a little too eager to kill. Did that mean he secretly wanted Dylan dead because of a little jealously? No.

Of course not.

Did it?

I mean, I didn't even know Dylan. We just met today.

"I see you're thinking about it. He doesn't seem so innocent now, does he?" Dylan sneered.

144

I glanced at Archer and saw that he was already looking at me. I couldn't help but freeze at the look he was giving me.

It was a look of hurt, maybe even a little sadness.

Why was he looking at me like that?

And then it hit me.

He was looking at me like that because he thought I truly believed Dylan.

Like I really thought he was some kind of monster.

Like I'd ever choose Dylan over him.

I opened my mouth to tell him the exact opposite, but once again, Dylan interrupted, "Come with me, Gemma. He's dangerous. Next thing you know, he'll be trying to kill you too. Whatever it takes so he can get out of here." Dylan held his hand out.

Did he actually expect me to take it?

Sure, Archer had killed some people down here, but they weren't normal or innocent in the first place. What he said was right. If he hadn't killed them, then we'd be dead instead. He practically saved us all.

Dylan was just starting to lose his damn mind down here.

I looked at Dylan's outstretched hand and then at him.

"No."

Dylan actually had the nerve to look shocked.

"What?"

"I said no."

"No? You're actually going to stay with him? You know what kind of guy he is! You saw it firsthand."

"I do, and I'm starting to understand what kind of guy you are too. You've gone off the deep end down here. The answer is and always will be no."

I grabbed on to Archer's hand and squeezed it.

Dylan looked about ready to combust.

He shook his head in frustration. "You're not thinking straight, Gemma. Come with me."

145

"No."

I watched as he clenched his fists and scoffed.

"Fine. If you don't want to come willingly, I'll have to force you but remember, I'm doing this to try and save you. You'll thank me for it eventually."

Dylan reached out before I could react and latched on to my free hand. He yanked me forward so fast that my hand was ripped free of Archer's, and I collided into his chest.

"Dylan, let her go," Archer said slowly, his voice low.

"No. I'm taking her with me. You'll only end up hurting her or worse."

"Like hell you are," I said. I swung my free hand forward and punched him square in the face.

It hurt like hell.

Dylan groaned and stumbled back.

He stepped so far back that he actually ended up losing his footing on the top step. Before I could even react, he had already lost his balance and was falling down the stairs.

I gasped and my hands flew to cover my mouth as I heard each thump as clear as day as his body hit each step until there was silence.

Oh my . . .

Did I just . . .

I felt a hand on my shoulder before I was spun around, and my face was pressed into Archer's chest.

I fisted his shirt in my hands.

"I didn't mean to—"

"You don't have to say anything." Archer's hold on me tightened.

I pulled back so I could look up at him.

"We have to go see if he's okay."

"Gemma—"

"No, we have to. He could be dead. I could've just killed him!"

"Gemma, listen to me. Once we find our way out of here, we'll call the police and let them deal with it."

"But Archer—"

"No buts. It was an accident, Gemma. He tripped and he fell. It's not your fault, and it's not your job to go and make sure that he's okay either. Especially not when he was just willing to basically kidnap you. We'll let the police handle it, okay?"

I glanced over my shoulder at the darkened set of stairs and swallowed hard before turning back to face Archer and nodded slowly.

"How are we going to get out of here?" I asked quietly.

"We could try kicking our way out like we did in the subway train," Archer joked, trying to lighten the horribly dark mood.

I quickly pulled away from Archer, then I snatched his phone out of his hand and shined the light on the wood that was blocking our way.

"Gemma, I was kidding."

"I know but you might be on to something. Look at the wood."

Archer came up next to me and looked at where I was shining the light.

"Do you see how it looks rotted in some places? I bet this wood has been here forever. It can't be too hard to kick off or pull apart."

I glanced up at him with a new sense of hope.

"On three?"

Archer nodded.

"On three."

CHAPTER THIRTY-ONE

"One."

"Two."

"Three!"

The wood was weaker than I had originally thought. It was so weak that when our feet collided with it, it gave so easily that our feet went straight through.

I pulled my foot free of the hole and got down on my hands and knees to peer through it.

The sight that greeted me almost had me in tears.

"Archer, look," I said quietly.

Archer knelt next to me and peered through the hole.

"I don't fucking believe it," Archer said, his voice just as quiet as mine.

Through the small hole, I could see the faint city lights of New York. There weren't many stars to see, but I could see the navy-blue sky, letting me know that it was night. I could also hear the faint honking of car horns in the distance, so that meant we couldn't be too far away from people.

"How long do you think we've been down here?"

Archer shrugged. "I don't know, but I'm sure as hell ready to leave." He stood up and proceeded to kick the wood over and over with renewed energy. I watched as pieces of rotted wood gradually fell away until there was a decent-sized hole that we could both fit through.

"You go first, and I'll grab the she-beast." Archer gestured to Rose, who was still sitting in the same spot, squirming and glaring at the both of us.

I nodded and carefully made my way through the hole. When I got out, I stood up and took a deep breath. It felt like it had been forever since I breathed in fresh air.

Well, as fresh as it could get in New York.

I turned in a slow circle, trying to figure out where we were.

There were a lot of old and abandoned buildings around that were boarded up just like the subway entrance had been, and it looked like the subway entrance had been right in the middle of it all.

A few seconds later, Archer was pushing a squirming Rose through. I grabbed her by her arms and pulled her the rest of the way through before sitting her on the ground. I'm pretty sure if she hadn't been gagged, she'd be pouting now.

She obviously didn't like being handed off from person to person like some old package.

Archer finally made his way out. When he stood up, he took a look around before he started laughing.

I frowned, thinking maybe he had gone off the deep end too.

"Why are you laughing?" I asked cautiously as I watched him with questioning eyes.

Archer turned to look at me with a smile so bright that it was almost contagious.

Archer rushed forward and scooped me up into his arms before spinning me around.

I yelped in surprise. When I was back on my feet, I looked up at Archer with a confused smile.

"What was that?" I said through a small laugh.

Archer had his hands wrapped around my waist and was still smiling brightly down at me.

"We're free. We're actually free. We did it." He sounded like he couldn't believe it. I had to admit, there were times—a lot of them actually—where I thought we wouldn't make it out either.

Standing here outside seemed surreal.

"I know," I said quietly.

Archer rested his forehead against mine with his eyes closed and inhaled deeply, almost like he was savoring the moment.

When he opened his eyes again, his smile had lessened a little.

"We should call the police," he suggested and I nodded.

Archer let go of me and quickly brought his phone up to his face and shook his head ruefully.

I looked at him with a frown. "What is it?"

"I would get a signal *now*."

I simply shook my head. If I had to bet, the whole no signal thing was probably those lunatics's doing too.

Archer quickly dialed a number and held the phone over his ear. As I stood there and listened to him give a brief rundown of the events to the operator, I couldn't help but realize how crazy it all sounded.

We really had been through hell.

When Archer hung up, he turned to me and gave a relieved sigh.

"The police are on their way."

For some reason, I suddenly started to feel the telltale stinging behind my eyes as tears started to form.

Archer, obviously thinking that something was wrong, hurried over to me with a concerned expression.

"What is it? What's wrong?"

I shook my head and took a step forward before wrapping my arms around him and burying my face in his shirt.

It wasn't until right then that all the events of our time spent down there came rushing back. I really didn't think we'd make it out alive.

Archer seemed to now understand and just held me silently while I cried.

When the tears stopped flowing, I pulled back and wiped the back of my hand across my eyes.

Archer slung one arm around my shoulder and silently led me to the curb of the abandoned street.

We sat there like that, just me, him, and a restrained eight-year-old, waiting for the police to arrive.

CHAPTER THIRTY-TWO

It took the police a while to arrive since we were practically in an abandoned part of New York now, but when they finally did arrive, everything was hectic.

There were at least ten police cars and three ambulances. I was even surprised when I saw that our local news station had shown up in their van. They hopped out with their cameras and microphones ready.

I felt like I was going to be sick.

I didn't know our situation had become so well known in such little time. Or maybe it hadn't been a little time. Maybe we had been down there longer than I originally thought.

I wasn't exactly keeping track of time while I was fighting for my life.

The paramedics were the first to reach us, and Archer and I were instantly torn apart.

One of the paramedics—a man probably in his late twenties with sandy blond hair and blue eyes—kneeled down in front of me with a red medical bag in his hand.

"You must be Gemma Conners," he said, his voice kind.

I nodded slowly. "How did you know?"

The paramedic chuckled. "Your picture has been up on almost all the local news stations since yesterday morning."

My eyes grew wide at that bit of information.

First off, we'd been down there for almost two days?!

How many times had I joked with my parents that taking the subway would end up with me being kidnapped and my picture on the news?

I *really* hoped they didn't use my high school ID picture.

If I hadn't been through what I had, I probably would've laughed at the whole thing.

The paramedic continued to talk while he rummaged through his bag and checked me over. "Your parents really care about you. They've been on the news begging for your return. They offered up a pretty large amount of money too and all in less than forty-eight hours. They must know some important people."

Unexpected tears filled my eyes at the thought of my parents. I couldn't imagine what they had been going through.

And then, another thought suddenly popped up.

"You said they even offered a reward?" I asked.

The paramedic nodded as he slowly dabbed a cotton pad against my forehead, which stung like hell. "Yep."

They better not have offered up my college fund.

We were going to have to talk about this.

When would I see them?

As soon as that thought crossed my mind, I heard the screech of tires against asphalt as a car came to a stop.

I looked up to see two cars—a silver Porsche and a black Jeep Cherokee—just as they skidded to a stop.

I watched as my mom and dad rushed out of the Jeep and headed towards me while two other people—who I'm assuming were Archer's parents—quickly climbed out of the Porsche and rushed towards him.

"Gemma!" I heard my mom wail. The next thing I knew, both she and my dad were kneeling on the ground, pulling me into a tight embrace and smothering me with kisses, but I didn't mind, at least not this time. I had missed them so much. I honestly thought that I might never get to see them again.

When they finally pulled back, they both had tears in their eyes.

"Oh, my poor baby. What happened to you? When we got the call from your school yesterday morning saying that you hadn't shown up, we didn't know what to think," my mom said, her voice shaking.

"You didn't . . . y-you didn't run away, did you? Is something going on? If—" my dad started.

"No! I'd never run away. I have no reason to," I cut my dad off.

"Is that what you guys thought? That I ran away because I wasn't happy at home?" I asked quietly.

"We thought that maybe we had done something," my mom said.

I shook my head. "You guys didn't do anything. Besides, I couldn't run away even if I wanted to. I can't cook. I'd starve to death, and we all know how I feel about my food."

Teary smiles appeared on both my parent's faces and I smiled back.

"So what happened to you?" my dad asked.

I opened my mouth to reply but the paramedic interrupted, "I'm sorry but we should really get her to the hospital so she can be properly checked."

My parents nodded. When another paramedic came over with a stretcher, I let them lift me up on to it and roll me over to the nearest ambulance. Once inside, I took a look outside.

The flashing lights of the police cars and ambulances bathed everything in red and blue.

I watched as a few policemen completely tore away the boarded-up entrance of the subway station and then made their way down into it.

I shivered, knowing they would find Dylan first, who I wasn't sure was dead or not, and a lot of other bodies down there.

154

When one of the policemen came back up and rushed over to a group of paramedics by an empty ambulance and they quickly followed with a stretcher, I knew Dylan was probably alive. Otherwise, they would've been heading down there with a body bag.

Next, I turned my attention to a man and woman, who were both hugging a now uncuffed and ungagged Rose.

I frowned at that but decided not to worry about it.

She wasn't my problem anymore.

"You ready, sweetie?" I looked up as my mom climbed up into the ambulance and took a seat next to the stretcher.

I nodded. "Where's Dad?"

"He's going to follow in the car."

I nodded again, and just before the doors of the ambulance closed, I caught sight of Archer in an ambulance opposite of the one I was in with that stupid grin on his face—the same grin that had started to grow on me.

He gave a dramatic wave, the kind you saw the girls do in old movies when their husbands went off to war, and I couldn't help but laugh.

I returned the wave, just as dramatic, and watched as his grin turned into a soft smile to match my own before the doors of the ambulance were closed.

CHAPTER THIRTY-THREE

Three Weeks Later

"That's not it."

"It is."

"It isn't."

"I think, of all people, I'd know best and I'm telling you that's not it."

"And I'm telling you that it is."

"Fine, why don't we let *her* tell us then?"

"Fine."

We both faced forward, waiting for the girl in question to give us our answer.

A few seconds passed and then . . .

"My favorite part of the day was when we climbed the big red hill, and once we got to the top, it turned out to be the big red chicken and we all danced together!"

I spun around and punched Archer in the shoulder. "Ha! I told you that was going to be her favorite part!"

Yes, we were watching *Dora the Explorer*.

It may or may not have become our thing after Archer had given me the nickname while we were lost down there.

It had been a little over three weeks since the incident on the subway, and I was sitting in the living room of Archer's freakishly large house, dressed in a pair of gray sweats, a tank top, and a pair of hot pink fuzzy socks watching *Dora the Explorer* with Archer while both our parents cooked in the kitchen.

I never thought I'd see the day that my parents and I would be having dinner with Archer and his parents.

The first few days after the incident were chaotic to say the least. At the hospital, it was revealed that I had a few bruised ribs, one dislocated shoulder, a minor concussion, and other minor cuts and bruises. My parents refused to leave my side.

The day I was released and went home, I just wanted to relax and be left alone, so I went to my room to watch some mindless show on TV. The only problem was that when I turned on my TV, the first person I saw was Rose and the man and woman I saw hugging her before I was taken to the hospital.

They were talking about how traumatic the whole experience was for them to some reporter. It turned out that the man and woman were her real parents and Rose had actually been reported missing over a month ago.

That little bit of information ruined my whole day. I spent the whole day wondering, if those were Rose's real parents, then how did she get mixed up with Dox? Did he kidnap her? And why did she call him Daddy then? What had he done to her?

To make things even worse, Dylan and his family were trying to sue mine.

Yes, Dylan was alive, and apparently, he had made the whole thing out to be my fault. He blamed me for all of his injuries and claimed that I tried to lead him to his death because I grew infatuated with him while we were down there and he didn't feel the same way. Those were his *exact* words.

On a more positive note, Archer didn't go to jail on three counts of murder like I had secretly thought he might since the whole thing *was* self-defense.

On top of that, the remaining guy who had been with Dox was captured not long after the incident.

Unfortunately, that still left one that was unaccounted for, but I didn't try to think about that.

The ending theme music to *Dora* cut on and I jumped up and down yelling, "I was right!" I continued to do so until I felt satisfied with myself and slumped back down on the couch with a smile on my face.

"Yeah, real mature," Archer teased before sticking his tongue out at me.

I rolled my eyes. "Oh yeah, you're definitely the mature one in this relationship."

"I am." Archer crossed his arms and pouted.

I crawled over so I was right next to him and pinched one of his cheeks. "Aww, is the baby upset?"

Archer smacked my hand away and narrowed his eyes at me, but I could see he was fighting off a smile.

"Don't be such a baby. Eventually, you'll learn to live with the fact that I'm always right, even when I'm wrong."

Archer gave me a flat look and continued to say nothing.

"Are you really going to sit there and say nothing?" I asked after a full minute of nothing but silence.

Still no answer.

Fine.

Two could play this game.

I sighed dramatically and stood up so I was standing right in front of him.

"I guess I'll just go get in the hot tub then and try on that new bikini I bought while you sit here and pout." I stood up and started toward the hall that would lead me to the indoor pool, which also held the hot tub—once I found out that Archer had a hot tub in his house, it was hard to tear me away from it for long periods of time—but before I could make it to the hall, I felt Archer wrap his arms around my waist and pull me back into his chest.

"I'm done pouting now. I'll be a good boy," Archer whispered in my ear.

I laughed and spun around before placing my hands on his chest.

"Hmm, I don't know. I don't think I can take your word for it. You'll have to convince me."

Archer's signature smirk spread across his lips.

"I think I can do that."

Archer leaned down and his lips had just brushed against mine when a familiar voice called out, "Move one more inch and I'll feed you to the dog."

Archer stepped away from me so fast you would've thought I'd slapped him.

I watched as Archer rubbed the back of his neck nervously and looked down at the ground before mumbling a quick, "Um, hi, Mr. Conners."

I sighed and turned to face my dad.

"Dad, we don't even have a dog," I pointed out.

"Yes, but I can buy one."

"But you're allergic."

"Then I'll buy a lion."

My dad pointed two of his fingers to his eyes and pointed it to Archer, doing the "I'm watching you" gesture before he spun around and headed back to the kitchen.

"Your dad is going to kill me," Archer deadpanned.

I shook my head. "You should be more worried about my mom."

I walked back over to the couch and fell back against the cushions.

Archer followed and sat down next to me.

"Do you think you're ready for tomorrow?" he suddenly asked.

I sighed heavily before dropping my head on his shoulder.

Tomorrow was the day that I'd be heading back to school. After the subway situation, Archer and I were allowed two weeks off from school to "recover" but my parents were convinced I needed an extra week of recovery before I was ready to head back there.

Megan came by my house every other day with all the work I missed in class so I wouldn't fall behind after demanding to know every little detail of what happened while I was down there. The funny thing was that she wasn't talking about the whole hostage situation. She wanted to know about me and Archer—after she found out that I was okay, of course.

I kept telling her I would tell her at school so that I'd have time to adjust to things myself, but the truth was, I wasn't sure if I was ready to go back to school just yet, and I wasn't just saying that because I hated school in general. After what happened on the subway, I began to have nightmares and with school being number two on my list of top places to sleep, I was scared that I might start having them there.

"I don't know," I answered and started messing with the hem of my shirt.

"Gemma."

I picked up the remote and began randomly flicking through the channels on TV.

"Yeah?" I answered, pretending to be interested in my channel surfing.

Archer took the remote out of my hand so I was forced to look at him.

"You're not ready to go back." It wasn't a question.

I hugged my knees to my chest and shook my head. "I'm starting to have nightmares, almost every night now," I said quietly.

I was afraid to look up and see Archer's face.

"I'm starting to think that I might be going crazy or something. I keep reliving what happened down there and nothing is helping. I've been to the doctor about a million times in the last

160

few weeks and the stupid sleeping pills aren't working, and I don't know what to do. I can't even go outside without thinking that some creep is going to kidnap me. I have to hide it from my parents now because I don't want to worry them anymore than I already have, but I-I can't keep—"

Archer pulled me to him and wrapped his arms tightly around me.

I buried my head in the front of his shirt and shut my eyes tight.

I could feel myself shaking and my breathing had increased.

Was I having a panic attack?

"I have them too," Archer said quietly.

I waited for the shaking to stop before I looked up at him.

"What?"

"The nightmares, I have them too. They started the same night we made it out. It was only one or two every few days, but now, I'm starting to have more of them."

"Do your parents know?" I asked.

Archer shook his head.

"No one knows. Well, no one except you now."

I leaned forward and laid my head on his chest again.

Archer rested his chin on top of my head and tucked a piece of hair behind my ear. "We'll get through this, Gemma."

We sat like this—with Archer's arms wrapped around me while I rested my head on his chest—until Archer's mom called us for dinner.

*　　　*　　　*

Later That Night

It was a little after midnight and I was laying on my bed, staring up at the ceiling. After dinner at Archer's house, my parents and I headed home, and I instantly retreated to my room.

161

I was exhausted, but I refused to go to sleep because I knew what would happen if I did.

My vision had actually started to blur from staring at the ceiling for so long when a sharp tapping sound came from outside my window.

My heart started pounding furiously against my chest as I quickly sat up and threw the covers off before instantly looking around my room for a weapon.

The closest thing was my math book, which sat on my desk, so I grabbed it and silently crept over to my window.

With one hand gripping the math book, I used the other to pull the curtains back a little to try and see outside but it was too dark to see anything.

I took a deep breath and mentally counted down.

One . . .

Two . . .

Three . . .

I threw the curtains back and yanked the window up in a flash, and to my surprise, Archer was standing there, or rather, he was lying there. I opened the window so fast that he fell straight into my room and landed on the floor.

"You almost gave me a heart attack!" I whisper-yelled, mindful of my parents.

Archer grunted and stood up.

"Why? Were you expecting someone else tonight?" he asked with raised eyebrows.

I scoffed and rolled my eyes.

"Yeah, actually, I was. *Jace Wayland* should be here *any* minute now."

Archer frowned at that. "Who the hell is *Jace Wayland?*"

I simply shook my head at him. It was then that Archer noticed the math book in my hand.

"Let's say it hadn't been me outside your window. What did you plan on doing? Boring somebody to death?"

"Oh, ha-ha. You're hilarious," I mumbled before tossing the book on my bed, then sitting on the edge myself.

"What are you doing here anyway?" I asked.

Archer closed my window before he came and laid down on his back next to me.

"Couldn't sleep," he said simply.

I crossed my legs and stared at him.

"So you decided to drive to my house in the middle of the night because you couldn't sleep? You do know we have school tomorrow, right?"

"Yep, nice pajamas, by the way."

I looked down at what I was wearing and felt my face heat up.

I wasn't expecting anyone to come crashing through my bedroom window at midnight, so I was only dressed in a white camisole and a pair of pink Tweety Bird pajama shorts.

I grabbed my pillow and placed it on my lap to try and cover my shorts.

Archer laughed and then grinned at me. "So what were you up to?" he asked.

"Oh, didn't you know? I'm into this new thing where I actually try and go to sleep in the middle of the night."

Archer gave me a flat look and said, "Your sarcasm does not amuse me."

I grabbed another pillow from the head of my bed and threw it so it landed right on his face. "Yeah, well, *that* amuses me," I said, laughing.

Archer took the pillow from his face and sat up slowly, then he turned to face me.

I saw the mischievous glint in his eyes, and before I had time to get up, Archer had already launched forward and grabbed me around the waist, causing us to fall backwards.

Archer grinned at me and suddenly started wiggling his fingers on my sides.

163

I couldn't help the burst of laughter that escaped as I started squirming around.

"Archer, s-stop!" I said through fits of laughter. "You're going to wake up my—"

My sentence was cut off as Archer started tickling me harder, and I burst into another fit of laughter.

"Say you're sorry and I'll stop."

"Stop, you're going to make me pee!"

"I'm not stopping until you say sorry."

"Okay, okay! I'm sorry."

A self-satisfied smirk came across Archer's face as he finally let go of my sides.

I took a deep breath and then glared up at him.

"You're lucky my parents didn't wake up." And then as an afterthought, I added, "And you almost made me pee on myself."

"You shouldn't have thrown the pillow at me."

"Jerk."

"You love me."

"I love my bed and food. Last time I checked, you were neither of those."

Archer sighed dramatically and rolled off me so he was standing up now. "Well, I guess I'll just go back home while you sit here and pout then."

Was he using the hot tub trick on me?!

Archer started towards the window, and I quickly sat up. Before I could stop myself, I opened my mouth to stop him. "Wait."

Archer turned around slowly, a cocky smile on his stupid good-looking face. "Hmm?"

I groaned and asked, "Are you really going to make me say it?"

"You know I am."

I sighed heavily.

"Will you stay with me?"

"Hmm, I don't know. You'll have to convince me."

He was definitely getting back at me for the hot tub incident earlier, but surprisingly enough, I found that I didn't mind.

I stood up, made my way over to him, and wrapped my arms around his waist before looking up at him.

"Archer, will you stay with me? Please?" I asked, my voice soft.

All traces of that cocky smile disappeared off his face, replaced by something more intense as he stared at me.

He swallowed once before nodding.

I gave him a small, appreciative smile. "Thank you."

Archer stared down at me for a few more seconds before leaning down and bringing his lips to mine.

It felt like my first kiss with him all over again.

You know, minus the burning subway car.

I pressed my body up against his and his arms slowly slid around me. One hand was pressed against my lower back and the other was cupped behind my neck.

I slowly ran my fingers through his hair and was rewarded with a low groan from him.

Archer started trailing kisses down my jaw and then to my neck.

"Archer," I whispered breathlessly.

I wasn't really sure where this was headed; waking my parents up was suddenly the last thing on my mind now.

His whispered name seemed to spur something in him because the next thing I knew, he was gently pushing me backwards until my back met my bed, and he was hovering over me.

Archer was staring at me with a small smile on his face.

"What?" I asked through a nervous laugh.

"You don't know how long I've thought about this."

"You've been thinking about breaking into my house in the middle of the night to make out with me? Should I be worried?" I asked teasingly.

Archer rolled his eyes and shook his head. "You know what I mean. I've always thought about being with you."

An unfamiliar feeling started in my chest and stomach.

Was I having a heart attack?

I hoped not.

I decided to ignore it for the moment and pulled his head back down to mine.

We were doing too much talking.

*   *   *

I laid in my bed with Archer right next to me, his arm draped across my side.

If you were wondering if we did it, the answer would be no.

We kept it PG-13.

Mostly.

"You know if my parents catch you, you're dead," I said quietly, but the truth was, I really didn't care who walked in on us at the moment. This was the safest I'd felt in three weeks.

Archer leaned forward and kissed me lightly on the forehead. "Yeah, but it'll be worth it."

And it was. That night, for the first night since the subway incident, I slept comfortably and without any nightmares or worrying about whether or not someone was after me.

Archer was right. We would get through this.

Together.

*

*

*

Do you like thriller stories?
Here are samples of other stories
you might enjoy!

Psycho Sitter

Alexandria Ayers

PROLOGUE

I started tapping my fingertips on the steering wheel as I waited outside her house. Her parents should be leaving soon, so it wouldn't be too long now. I tried to focus on planning what I was going to do, but all that seemed to fill my mind was how stupid the young girl's parents are. Hiring a sitter online isn't always dangerous, but if you're ignorant enough not to check the reviews on the website, and at least ask for background checks, then you're asking for trouble.

As far as her mother and father knew, they were waiting for Susan Kelly, a forty-six-year-old woman and a loving and caring mother of four, with a degree in nursing and only three speeding tickets on her record. But little did they know that a storm had headed their way. Of course, that storm was devilishly handsome and is known as me. Who else would it be?

"How much longer do you think it'll be before they leave?" Lane asked, resting his head on the steering wheel. His car was parked only a few feet away from mine.

"Shouldn't be too much longer," I replied, glancing over at the house. We had to park behind a bundle of trees on the other side of a small field that's between us and the house. I swear, these people live in the middle of nowhere. If anything were to happen, they would be screwed — plain and simple. Why would they even want to live in the country, anyway? There's nothing to do, and on top of that, it smells like shit. Hell, I wouldn't be surprised if we were smelling actual shit.

"I'm hungry. Can we come back later? Or how about we just skip out on this one? I'm tired." Lane groaned.

"If you're really that hungry and tired, then leave, because there's no way I'm skipping out on this one. Phil would have my head if he knew I didn't bring one back. I need to keep up with my reputation." I glanced at him with annoyance. It's tiring having to explain this to him — especially since I've told him only about a million times already.

Phil was our boss, and I knew the moment he handed me her file, I needed to have her. I had to be the one to bring her in. She was mine from the moment my eyes saw her bright, forest green ones.

"Fine. You have fun. I'm getting something to eat then head back to the field."

After Lane left, my thoughts started to drift on how she would react. Would she come willingly? Fight me and threaten to kill me? Or would she be just confused and almost unsure on how to react? I've seen all of them. Tears, rage, unsureness. It's always those three. I'd learned that much over the years of being in this... well you can call it a "unique" business.

Some people say this job is sick or twisted. Sometimes they'd ask, "Why would you want to work there, you sick freak?"

But they don't know that feeling I get when I see the fear and confusion written on the features of the unlikely young girls, who happened to fall into the trap of sex trafficking, or what we like to call pleasuring; the rich likes to call it shopping.

For the customers, it truly is just like going in the store and buying a toy. You pick the one you fancy, and after that, you pay. There's a catch, though. With this job, you get to keep the merchandise for only one night. Also, you can't keep the baby dolls. They're far too precious. That's what I tell the people who don't understand my job.

I saw movement in the house. It looked like the parents were leaving. I could just make out, what I assume, was the mother embracing her children then letting go just a bit too soon because of her husband pulling her away. This would be the last time she would hold her children in her arms. It's a shame they didn't hug longer.

As they got into their car, they sped down the old country road. I'm guessing they're running late for their flight.

Instead of driving up towards the home and barging inside, I decided that I'd wait for a while and let the thought of their sitter no longer coming to linger around.

Lane had probably made it back by now and, most likely, stuffed his face with only God knows what. I wonder if he'd be flying back to London tonight. I kind of hope he does, so he'd be out of my way. Plus, I didn't want him coming back here and trying to help me bring her in. She's mine, not his. I called the shots.

At first I saw her eyes, then I saw her. Her picture in the school yearbook, which Phil gave me, told me a lot about her appearance. She's beautiful. I have to say, she'll sell great, meaning an even bigger check for me. Gorgeous, more money. Double hit. Lucky me.

The only thing that is so annoying about her is that her brother is with her. I was still debating on what I could do to the little brat. Maybe I should just leave him here? No, he'd just call the cops and get my ass hauled to jail, even though he's only a kid. I'm already in enough trouble. If the Feds find out about this job, I'll be locked up for, no telling, how many years.

I'll have to think of something because I can't take the dipshit with me. I'm afraid to even think of what Phil would do if I brought in a boy. He'll probably think I'm nuts and cut my check. There's no way I'd let him do that. I work too hard not to get paid less than what I already do. Anyway, he knows that he shouldn't mess with me. I bring in most of the girls, so he can't do a thing to me unless he wants to lose his best employee.

After sitting in the car for a few more hours, I couldn't stand it anymore. I needed to go and get her. I opened the SUV door, jumped out, and headed towards the home. After making sure I had my gun and pocket knife in my jacket, I exited the vehicle. The crisp January air pierced through my thin clothes as I treaded on the snow-blanketed ground.

Before I reached the entrance, I noticed that all the lights in the house seemed to be turned off. Maybe they knew I was coming? No, that's not possible. It's pitch black out here, there's no way they could have seen me.

I shrugged it off and headed for the front door. After knocking three times, I pulled out a cigarette, placed the hazardous paper stick between my lips, and leaned on the door frame. A minute passed before a young boy opened the door, fear written all over his face.

"Hello," I spoke, looking down at the boy.

Seconds later, she appeared.

I was met with long, unruly hair and bright, green eyes, staring at me suspiciously. The picture in that file really did her no justice. A slender figure with slim torso and compelling legs. There's no denying it — she's hot as hell. It's been a long time since I've seen someone with a body like hers.

She shielded her brother. She placed herself in front of him as she watched me light a second cigarette. I brought it to my lips and breathed out the smoke. I wonder if the reason that she's looking at me with a worried face—which still looks hot—had something to do with the fact that I looked like a psychopathic murderer, or she could somehow see the money signs on my eyes.

"Who are you and what do you want?" Her mellifluous voice echoed across the empty fields.

It hadn't been that long yet, but I was already intrigued.

CHAPTER 1

CASSANDRA

I was walking down the halls of Britwood High School with my best friend Summer. As I opened the door to the parking lot, the cool January air hit my face, making a shiver run down my back. The ground was covered with a blanket of snow, making it look like a winter wonderland.

"Are you listening to me?" Summer's voice broke my thoughts.

"W-what? Oh, um..." I stuttered.

"I asked, what you're doing later. I thought maybe we could hang out."

"I told you earlier, my parents are leaving for Australia tonight, and the sitter is coming, so I can't have friends over," I said.

"Oh yeah. But I can come over later this week, right?" she asked, opening her car door.

"Well my parents said no friends over this week because I'm in trouble," I said, looking down at the ground.

"What'd you get into trouble for?"

"For not picking up Ben from school. He was left standing outside the school when it was below freezing," I said, looking down, ashamed.

Summer started laughing and clapping her hands.

"You forgot your own brother when it was below freezing?"

"Yeah..."

"Is that why you have to have a sitter?" she asked, finally able to control her laughter.

"Yeah, they said if I couldn't even remember to pick up my own brother from school, then there was no way they were leaving him with me for a week."

"Well I wouldn't either," Summer said, getting in her car.

"Bye! See ya later." she shouted before closing her door.

I yelled a bye back then got in my piece of junk, my truck, and pulled out of the school parking lot.

* * *

I got out of my truck and headed for the front door.

"I'm home!" I yelled from the door, kicking off my shoes and taking off my coat.

"I'm in here!" I heard my mother's voice call from the kitchen.

I walked into the kitchen, where I saw my mother preparing some kind of soup.

"I'm making you, Ben, and the sitter some potato soup," she said, stirring the so called "soup."

My mother was never a very good cook, but then again, neither was I.

"Speaking of the sitter, when will she be here?" I asked, stepping towards the gross-looking, chunky liquid.

"In about thirty minutes." I looked up at the clock above the sink to see that it was 5:30 pm.

"Well I better be getting my suitcase in the car," my mother said, and she headed upstairs.

I decided just to watch some TV.

* * *

"Now make sure to use your manners, do whatever she says, and be nice," my mother said.

I just rolled my eyes, I already knew to do that. I don't know why she had to tell us.

"Okay, I love you," she said, giving my little brother, Ben, a huge hug then gave me one.

I didn't really hug back, I was still mad at her for not trusting me with Ben. Yes, I know I forgot about picking him, but I didn't mean to. She just doesn't have faith in me.

"I love you, guys. The sitter should be here in a few minutes. You think you can handle Ben?" Mom asked, looking straight at me.

"Yes, mom, I'm pretty sure I can handle him for a few minutes," I said, annoyed.

"We love you, and we'll see you two in a week," Dad said, trying to get my mother to leave before they missed their plane.

"Bye, love you." Mom said as Dad shut the front door.

I turned around to look at Ben and said, "What do you wanna do, brat?"

"I'm hungry, poophead." Ben has been calling me that for years. He says it's because my hair color looks a lot like "poop".

"There's soup on the stove," I said, going to the kitchen.

"Did mom cook it?" He sounded kinda worried because he knew mom couldn't cook.

"Yeah, she did." I said, smiling, as I opened the door of the fridge, got out some leftover pizza, and put it on a plate.

"Please," Ben said, looking up at me with puppy dog eyes.

"Please what?" I spat, looking down at the blond-haired boy.

"Share. I don't want to eat mom's chunky soup,'" he said, looking at the two slices of pizza on the paper plate.

"No way," I said, walking to the living room.

"Please, Cassie."

He said, grabbing my arm. I looked down at him only to see tears in his blues eyes. Great, I made him cry.

"Fine." I gave him a slice.

"Yes!" He took the piece, ran, and jumped on the couch. "That little rat," I thought.

We watched TV for a couple of hours until we noticed it was already eight o'clock. I was wondering if that sitter was even coming. Maybe she got lost or something. It was dark outside, and sometimes it could be hard to see the road signs. Just then the TV shut off, along with the lights, leaving us sitting in the dark.

"Cass, what's going on?" Ben said, hugging onto my side.

"I don't know—" A knock on the door made me and Ben both jump back.

"Don't move," I said slowly. The knock on the door got louder.

"Maybe it's the sitter," Ben said, still holding onto me for dear life. He hates the dark. He'll do anything not to be in the dark.

"Maybe," I said.

"Maybe they can turn the lights back on," he said and ran towards the door.

"No Ben!" I yelled, running after him.

It was too late, though, he had already unlocked and opened the door.

"Hello," a deep raspy voice said.

I grabbed Ben and put him behind me. The only thing I could really see about the man standing in front of me was that he was tall and had a cigarette between his lips. I squinted, trying to see more of him. He put his hand in one of his pockets as he pulled out an object. I didn't know what it was till he moved his finger down on it, making a small flame ignite out of the silver hole.

I could now see his face. He had brown, curly hair that was swiped over to one side, an eyebrow ring, and a lip ring. He had tattoos running up on his neck, but that's not what caught my attention the most. It was his piercing green eyes. They were so beautiful and captivating.

"Take a picture. It'll last longer, babe." His deep voice snapped me out of my thoughts.

He walked past me and into the house, looking around like he was trying to find something, even though he could barely see anything because the lights were out.

"What are you doing?" I spoke for the first time since he showed up.

"Looking for the basement." I stopped in my tracks. Why would he want to know where the basement was?

"W-why?" I stuttered, scared of the answer.

"To tie you up and put you down there."

If you enjoyed this sample, look for
Psycho Sitter
on Amazon.

DEMENTED

SINISTER TALES

ANNA GALLEGOS

A SON'S RAGE

A story about a son's disturbing thoughts and wicked desires turned into evil actions.

"James!" My mother's voice roared through the whole house, bouncing off the walls. What was she mad about this time? Something stupid, I thought.

"Get your ass down here!"

Letting a sigh escape from my lips, I trudged downstairs to face what punishment she had for me. Was it going to be hair pulling or a frying pan to the face? I wouldn't know. It always caught me off guard even though I expected it.

My fingers slid against the railing of the stairs, noticing how smooth it was. I looked everywhere but at my mom. Even though I wasn't staring into those soulless eyes of hers, I knew she had anger written on her face. I couldn't remember the last time I've seen a real smile on her face, not the fake one she puts on when guests are over. If only they knew of the evil that lived in that woman. Maybe they'd take me away and put me in a better home. That'd be nice.

I looked down at my bare feet. They seemed much more interesting than dealing with my mom.

I looked up for a second and stared into the eyes of the woman that stood before me, the woman I called mom. She didn't deserve that title, she wasn't much of a mom. What kind of mother puts down her own son every chance she gets?

Her eyes pierced through me, for a split second fear struck me. I quickly pushed away that emotion, no longer would I be afraid of her. Soon, all worries of this terrible woman would be gone and I'd be put at peace.

"I got a call from school today," she managed to say through clenched teeth, her hands curled into fists. I took a step forward to show that she couldn't make me cower in fear anymore.

"And?' I asked. I had no idea what in the world she was talking about.

She was pissed, and the expression on her face proved I was right.

"They said you weren't in class today." She took a step forward without any hesitation. She wasn't going to win this war.

"I was in school today." I gave her a dumbfounded look. I wasn't lying, I was definitely in all my classes today. I wanted to graduate so I could get away from this hell hole.

I don't know how the school would get that wrong. I wasn't tardy to any of my classes today. It had to be a mistake, but I knew all the convincing in the world wouldn't make her believe me. She always wanted a reason to start a fight; always wanted a reason to smack me around.

"Are you saying that they're lying? Why would they lie, James?" she cocked her head at me, anger still burning up in her.

"I don't know." I shrugged my shoulders, proceeding to look back at my feet. "Maybe they made a mistake."

I don't know why I'm trying to convince her that I didn't skip. She wouldn't believe me. She always called me a rotten child, a child she never wanted, a child she wished she had given up when she had the chance.

"Stop lying to me!" she yelled, and her fist collided with my left cheek bone.

I fell to the polished wooden floor, my vision blurred in and out for a few seconds before a pounding headache came in.

Using my hands, I propped myself up to my knees, then grabbed a chair nearby to help me up.

By the time I got up, I noticed little drops of blood dripping from my mouth to the ground. My anger grew worse, but I held it back. I needed to save this anger for another time, a time when I plan to turn my thoughts into actions.

I didn't bother to look at the smug expression on her face. As I walked back up to my room, my breathing became harder and my fists clenched. I walked into my room, slamming and locking the door behind me. I didn't care if she hit me. After a while, I got used to the pain. It was like my face was numb forever; like I could no longer feel the burning pain that she inflicted on my face.

I tried to fall asleep for the longest time but I couldn't, so I just looked out my window. I saw that it was starting to get dark. The light post at the back of our house turned on, giving the yard a little bit more light.

I couldn't sleep knowing that the horrid beast was still breathing. She didn't deserve to live another second on this earth. My hate for her only grew stronger the longer I thought about it.

The stars twinkled outside. I wish I were one. I bet stars didn't have to deal with any of this at all. All they had to do was shine brightly in the sky while people stared at them with amusement and awe. People love stars. Love— that was a feeling I haven't felt in a while, not in years.

Tonight was the night.

It's perfect. No one's home except for me and my dear mother who I want dead so badly.

I walked over to my closet, carefully opening it so it wouldn't make so much noise. I grabbed everything I needed: duct tape, rope, a knife, a hand saw, and a lighter. I planned this for the past year and now, it was finally going to be put into action. I could already feel the weight of all the stress she had given me starting to fade away.

I felt numb. Not a second thought or feeling of guilt went through my head as I thought of the plan.

It was exactly eight o'clock when everything was ready. I descended the stairs, walking toward my mother's room. My heart fell in sync with my footsteps; I could feel it beating and pumping hard from excitement. Finally, I would be able to see her instead of me, being vulnerable. I was in charge this time and she couldn't stop me. She had no idea what fate has in store for her tonight. She would face my wrath. She would greet death's face soon. Maybe Satan wouldn't even want her and torture her down in hell forever. That'd teach her.

I grabbed the baseball bat that she kept by her bed every night, something that she thought would keep her safe from any unwanted visitors. With a tight grip on it, I smacked it across her head, knocking her unconscious. Now, I can proceed with my plan. After that hit, I felt a million times better. But I wasn't going to stop there. In fact, I felt even more encouraged to go through with my plan.

Blood dripped down the side of her head where the bat struck it. Red was a nice color on her, I'd like to see her wear more of it.

I wrapped my hand wrapped around her knotty hair, dragging her outside to the big tree that sat in the middle of our yard. I didn't have to worry about being caught or seen by anyone. The nearest neighbors were far enough that they wouldn't be able to know what was going on. She was always a sucker for privacy, and it worked in my favor.

As I tied her to the tree, I chanted the horrible things she said to me in my life. "You're worthless, James. I wish you were never born, James. I hate you, James. I never loved you. I wish I had given you up. You're lucky I didn't kick you out and let you live on the streets."

Saying those words out loud only added fuel to the burning anger inside me. They made me feel worse, imagining her saying them with a nagging voice. I tightened the rope around her hands without noticing it at first, but I didn't care. I didn't care if she lost circulation in her hands. She would soon be dead anyway.

Splashing some water on her, I saw her eyes flicker open and check her surroundings. I could tell she was scared. It was the exact reaction I imagined and hoped for. When her eyes landed on me, she looked dismayed, like she didn't believe what she was seeing.

Before she even tried to talk, I smacked some duct tape across her mouth. I didn't care for what she had to say anymore. She brought this on herself. If only she had changed sooner, she would not be in this situation now. I gave her plenty of chances, but now all her chances were gone. Soon, she would be gone from my life and I wouldn't have to worry anymore.

I took the lighter out of my pocket and flicked it to life. I was thankful it wasn't windy or rainy tonight. I used my left hand to hold the hand saw over the lighter. The heat of the fire glided up the knife, making the blade hot. I grabbed her hand, looking down at her wrist before I brought the saw to it. Her flesh sizzled as I cut into her, blood spurting from the wound. The further I cut into her wrist, the more I could see the insides. It beckoned me to cut deeper.

I closed my eyes before I completely chopped off her wrist... I wanted to savor her muffled screams. It brought me joy—something I hadn't felt in a long time because of her. But now, she brought the happiness back.

I was so lost in thought that by the time I opened my eyes, I didn't realize I had already cut her wrist entirely. The saw became soaked in her blood and bits of flesh stuck to it. Then, I began to work on the next wrist. I flicked the lighter to heat up the hand saw again until I thought it was ready for another round. She began to lose consciousness. I couldn't have that. I picked up her chopped-off hand and smacked her across her face with it. "No. No time for sleep. You have to be awake for this." My voice was calm and collected, opposite to how she was acting. She was spazzing out and crying. I had to say, she was one ugly crier.

I grabbed the saw and heated it up again. I brought it to her wounds to stop the bleeding. The sizzle reminded me of the times we would go to the Japanese grill and watch the sushi chefs cook our food in front of us. They both sounded remarkably the same.

I brought down on her once again, sawing off her elbow. It cut through her skin with ease. The bone is always the toughest part, but I managed it. She deserved this, she needed to be punished. While working on her other arm, my own arms grew tired, but I pushed through. Who knew what kind of muscles I'd be getting from this?

Next, I worked on her feet. Feet always disgusted me. Just the thought of touching her dirty feet made me cringe but knowing she was going through hell made me push on. I sawed away her feet, thinking of it as sawing wood. She began to doze off again. This time, I slapped her with my own hand. The moon shone on her, showing the red mark my slap imprinted on her face.

After I cut off both her feet, I tossed them next to the others. Then, I worked on her legs. I ignited the lighter, ready to heat up the hand saw again. By now, the saw was a mix of black from the way I seared the blade and dark red from her blood. I sawed through a ton of flesh and muscle to get to the bone. I wondered if butchers found this as much fun as I did. I could feel everything—the cutting and digging of the saw as it got further into her.

When I was done with her limbs, I looked at my handiwork and a frown appeared on my face. It felt unfinished. Clearly I wasn't done yet. Something else needed to be done. My eyes scanned over her to see what more damage I could do that I hadn't already done.

I couldn't end her life until I was completely satisfied with what I had done. Her screams through the duct tape weren't enough for me anymore. Hearing the same sounds over and over again started to bore me. Also, the same old expressions of pain and discomfort on her face didn't seem to make me feel as good as I thought it would. I wanted the dullness to be gone. I needed the excitement back again.

So I started stabbing her repeatedly. As I did so, the blood splattered all over me as if I were a canvas. As I sliced her skin open, a feeling of happiness hit me again. The motivation grew and I wanted to do more to her. Cuts covered her body. I grinned at my handiwork.

I played with her blood that splashed from all the cuts I'd made. I soaked my fingers in the liquid, then I pressed them to my face. Feeling the gooey texture against my skin gave me a high, it made me feel like nothing had ever made me feel. When it dried, I continued with my work.

I lifted up the knife I hadn't used yet. The blade was clean and ready for slashing. I brought the knife to her throat to finish what I had started. It knife sliced through her skin like ice cream on a hot summer day. The crimson liquid gushed from the wound. Then I grabbed the hand saw to finish the job. I reached up to her head, pushing it against the tree as hard as I could. I sawed like a madman while staring into her eyes. The life was leaving her, I could see it but I didn't care. I could feel myself getting weary as I almost finished.

Her decapitated head fell to the ground and I felt a sense of relief. Her dead eyes stared in my direction. Still, her soulless eyes haunted me.

I left her amputated limbs lying there in the yard. I didn't care to bury any of the pieces because she didn't deserve a proper burial. Remorse, did I feel it? Not at all. I felt free, free of that evil demon.

"You could have changed." I said as I sat next to her limbs and body parts. "This could all have been prevented if you had changed. You're not my burden anymore. You belong to the devil himself, if even he wants to keep you. Goodbye, you pathetic waste of space." I finished my speech. My tired body wanted to be clean of her blood so I headed back to the house.

One of the buttons on the phone was blinking when I walked back inside, signaling there was some voicemail. I pressed it, leaving some drops of blood behind. A woman's voice spoke:

"Hi, you may remember me. We talked earlier, ma'am. It seems that I made a mistake. Your son was at school today. Sorry if it caused you any inconvenience. Have a nice night." And with that, the woman's voice was gone.

As I walked up the stairs to get cleaned off, I smiled.

If you enjoyed this sample, look for
Demented
on Amazon.

PSYCHO
BILLIONAIRE

KASHMIRA KAMAT

CHAPTER ONE

KIARA

The first time I ever saw him was during a long rainy night. The clock ticked 11 PM, which was cutting close to the restaurant closing time. Since it was a weekday, the restaurant barely had any customers.

I worked at a small Chinese restaurant called *Sea Dragon,* where we served the best chicken dumplings and roast egg rolls in town—at least that's what the restaurant was popular for, and people loved visiting here all the time.

My coworker, Kathy, had left early tonight because she had a date. She had requested me to cover for her, begging me with her puppy eyes, and I eventually gave in since Kathy usually did favors for me too.

Thus, I was left me alone with Diego who seemed to be mopping a puddle of Coke that a kid had spilled a few minutes back off the floor. He gave me a tired smile, a smile that indicated the impending doom of Friday, knowing full well that it was going to be hella crowded. We barely had time to breathe on a weekend.

We were almost done cleaning all the tables when suddenly, Sam, the chef walked out of the kitchen frantically. Worry was written all over his face. He had never seemed so agitated before, so this was clearly something serious.

"What's wrong, Sam?" I inquired.

"It's my daughter," he replied. "My wife was telling me on the phone that Lily is being rushed to the hospital because she's running a high fever. I . . . I need to go."

"You can't!" Diego interrupted. "It's still an hour before closing. What if there's another customer?" He threw me a look.

"Can't you guys just manage for one hour? Please." Sam's pleading eyes turned towards me. "I need to be with my daughter."

I nodded. "We will manage." I placed my hand on his back, giving it a reassuring pat. "You can go."

"What? Are you nuts?" Diego shrieked. "If Manager Jeff finds out, we are going to get our asses handed back to us. And we could get fired!"

"Jeff doesn't need to know," I said. "It's just one hour. No one's going to walk in at this time"

Diego sighed and resumed his work. His face was going red. It looked like he was going to burst a vein or two. Sam packed his stuff and stormed out of the door, thanking me for the millionth time.

I watched from the window as he settled into his old Honda Civic and pulled out of the parking lot.

Fifteen minutes after Sam left, the little restaurant bell dinged, indicating there was a customer. I knew that if it was just one person or perhaps a couple, I could manage, but in walked three men in suits and occupied a table near the window. One of them was Asian, the other was a lanky redhead, and the third, by the window, looked younger than the two.

I approached their table with a smile, and they probably noticed I didn't have a menu card in my hand.

"Gentlemen, actually we closed early tonight because the chef had to leave due to an emergency. We wouldn't be able to serve anything at the moment," I said. "I apologize."

"Maybe you haven't noticed, but the weather's bad outside, and there aren't many restaurants in this area, and most of them are closed," the attractive Asian explained. "Isn't there anything you can serve us?"

"Chicken fried rice and Wonton soup," I suggested. "That's the best I can make."

The group of men agreed to the suggestion. Feeling motivated to become the evening's chef for once; I rushed back into the kitchen, tied the apron around my waist, and began dicing the veggies.

Diego was nowhere in sight, probably sulking in the staff room at the back, having wanted nothing to do with my little adventure of serving the customers in the restaurant without a chef. He clearly did not trust my cooking skills.

I, for one, had always been observant of what Sam cooked and had tried his recipes at home a few times, and it had turned out good. Although I just knew a few things off the menu, it was enough to serve someone during desperate times like these.

A few minutes later, I served them their dinner. "Enjoy your meal," I said and resumed my work.

I noticed another man seated alone a few booths down. Diego had served him coffee and turned the *"Open"* sign to *"Closed"*

I could feel a pair of eyes boring into my back as I wiped the counter with a rag. I turned to look, and the young man from the trio was staring at me. He smiled, so I smiled back at him and looked away.

Something about his attitude gave me the creeps. I didn't dress sexy because I appreciated predators staring at my ass. It was part of my job. They told me putting on makeup usually earned a lot of tips, and yes, my coworkers were right. I knew it was appealing to some men to see women serving around dressed in a Chinese *Qipao*, and I received more compliments for it, but some men were downright pervy. That was what bothered me about this job.

The three men seemed to be enjoying the meal, and when it was time to pay, one of the men pushed his American Express card towards me, along with numerous hundred dollar bills.

"You're pretty good at cooking for someone who doesn't work as a chef," the dark-haired man said.

"Thanks," I said with a smile and then noticed the tip he had given me.

Four hundred dollars as tip? Either he hadn't noticed how much he'd given me or he was totally insane. The two men stared at him incredulously, and my jaw was probably on the floor too.

"It's for you. Don't be so surprised," he added.

"Are you sure?"

"Of course," he said.

A few seconds later, I gained my composure, and I knew that my face had lit up by then.

"Thank you so much, sir. I really appreciate it."

I was desperate, alright. I had bills to pay, my father's debts to clear, and a whole bag filled with responsibilities. It didn't help that my salary wasn't much, so the tips helped me a lot.

I pushed the money in my pocket and went as far as to see the customers out of the door as a polite gesture for their generosity.

After the coffee-drinking customer had paid and walked out, Diego and I were left to close the restaurant. He stayed at the cash counter to settle the bills while I took the trash out of the back door.

The storm had come to a halt. I placed some leftover fish and water for the stray cat that I had been feeding for over the past few months and started to make my way back inside the restaurant when a strong hand reached for the doorknob first and slammed the door shut.

I looked up to see who it was. The darkness made it quite difficult, but a flash of lightning allowed me to see that it was the same man as before. The man who'd generously tipped me.

I fidgeted. "Do you need anything?"

He straightened his blazer jacket and turned to look at his watch and smiled at me. "I can give you an extra two hundred," he suggested, smiling coyly. "What do you say?"

"I don't understand."

He sighed, took my hand in his, and placed it on the crotch of his pants, rubbing on it slightly, and groaned.

"I have my car parked just around the parking lot. We'll make it quick."

I snatched my hand out of his grasp, feeling disgusted. "I'm not a whore."

"Oh c'mon. I saw how you were smiling at me," he said as if that explained anything.

"I smile at all my customers. It doesn't mean anything." My voice was shaky by now.

"Just a quick fuck. You can do some exceptions for extra tips, right?"

I reached for my pocket and thrust the dollar bills in his face. "Here. I don't need your money. Now, move out of my way."

I should have known he was one of those creepy men who lured women by showing them the power of money. I shouldn't even have accepted such a hefty tip.

Stupid. Stupid. Stupid.

He let go of the door handle, so I opened the door and started walking in when he grabbed me out of nowhere, slammed the door, and locked it behind him. Next, he grabbed me and pushed me against the wall, ripping the top button off the dress.

I struggled, screaming for someone to help me when he covered my mouth with his palm. I heard my own muffled cries over the sound of thunder. I tried to knee his groin, and I may have scratched his cheek because it was now bleeding.

I smacked him, and he smacked me hard in return, muttering, *"stupid bitch"* under his breath. I was resisting so hard, but

I felt like I was going to lose the fight. I had this gut feeling that something bad was going to happen.

I realized this was the end; an ugly one where I would probably end up sexually assaulted and dead somewhere near the dumpster. They said you should never beg for mercy at the person causing an assault because begging usually fed their fantasy and made their experience even more fun, but I wasn't even in the state to think of all that.

I continued to repeat the words *"please"*. My dress was tattered and dirty from struggling on the ground. He had my wrists pinned down. His knee was nudging between my thighs as his hand made its way towards my panties when suddenly, he stopped.

I was brawling, trying to pull myself to a sitting position, covering myself and I dared to look towards him to see what had stopped the assault.

A man was standing in the alley. I couldn't see his face properly, but at that moment, I knew that he was my knight in shining armor.

If you enjoyed this sample, look for
Psycho Billionaire
on Amazon.

AUTHOR'S NOTE

Thank you so much for reading *The Subway*! I can't express how grateful I am for reading something that was once just a thought inside my head.

Please feel free to send me an email. Just know that my publisher filters these emails. Good news is always welcome.
jaejae@awesomeauthors.org

I'd love to hear your thoughts on the book. Please leave a review on Amazon or Goodreads because I just love reading your comments and getting to know you!

Can't wait to hear from you!

Jae Jae

ABOUT THE AUTHOR

Johnae' Jones (Jae Jae) is the author behind the first book in the short two book novel series "The Subway" which she started writing back during her Junior year in high school. Michigan born and raised, she now resides in Alabama where she attends school and devotes most of her time to writing and being a student.

Printed in Great Britain
by Amazon